To my Reisner kids,
who always make me feel
like a member of the family,

THE FIREBRINGER
AND OTHER
GREAT STORIES

THE FIREBRINGER
AND OTHER
GREAT STORIES

*Fifty-Five Legends That
Live Forever*

Retold by
LOUIS UNTERMEYER

*Illustrated by
MAE GERHARD*

M. Evans and Company, Inc., *New York*

This book for ROBIN, SHEILA, MARDI, LAUREL,
JONATHAN MICHAEL, *and* CRISTOPHER DAVID,
with grandfatherly love

ACKNOWLEDGMENTS

"Beatrice and the Statue" is freely adapted from *Sieben Legenden* by the Swiss author Gottfried Keller. It first appeared as "Sister Beatrice and the Statue" in *The Fat of the Cat* by Louis Untermeyer, copyright 1925, 1953, by Harcourt, Brace and Company. The story was extended into a dazzling spectacle, *The Miracle*, by the German producer Max Reinhardt; woven into a mystical play, *Sister Beatrice*, by the Belgian dramatist Maurice Maeterlinck; and made into "A Ballad of a Nun" by the English poet John Davidson.

"The Loreley" and "The Robber Baron" are from *Blue Rhine, Black Forest* by Louis Untermeyer, copyright by Harcourt, Brace and Company, 1930, 1958.

"Siegfried" is based on that part of the *Nibelungenlied* from which Wagner took episodes for his four-part music-drama *The Ring of the Nibelungs*. The story in this volume follows the version Wagner gave to the stage.

"Chanticleer" is a modernized prose rendering of most of Chaucer's "The Nun's Priest's Tale" from *The Canterbury Tales*.

"The Little Juggler" is a new treatment of a medieval story retold by Anatole France as "Our Lady's Juggler" and was made into Jules Massenet's opera, *The Juggler of Notre Dame*.

"Sybaris: The Life of Luxury" owes certain particulars to Trevor L. Christie's "The Lost City of the Sybarites" in *Saturday Review*, March 19, 1966.

For countless suggestions and editorial emendations, I am grateful to my wife, Bryna Ivens Untermeyer.

Library of Congress Catalog Card No. 68-18716
ISBN 0-87131-497-5 (Paperbound)

M. Evans and Company, Inc.
216 East 49 Street
New York, New York 10017

Manufactured in the United States of America

9 8 7 6 5 4 3 2 1

CONTENTS

Before You Read This Book

AS IN *The World's Great Stories* this volume includes tales that have lasted a long time and may well last as long as there are listeners. They are not fairy tales, although some are hard to believe. Most of them are records of events that actually happened or were said to have happened. A very few of these stories were created by individual authors; all the others belong to history, mythology, and folklore.

The present volume ranges through the centuries from the ancient to the medieval world and the age of romance. The tales come from Greece, Rome, France, England, Germany, Finland, Spain, Sicily, Switzerland, Scandinavia, Persia, India, and (a rather recent contribution) Alaska. They are legends that keep on living.

A legend is something that has not only been told but, transmitted from one narrator to another, has also been countlessly retold and often reshaped. In these retellings I have, in common with most story-tellers, used the language of my own day. Moreover, I have felt free to supply new details and add dialogues wherever they seemed appropriate. Refurbished and rephrased, the stories themselves remain (I hope) very much as they have come down to us, fresh, fascinating, and full of their essential vitality.

L. U.

THE FIREBRINGER

... *Prometheus*

HE LONG war between the fearful Titans and the Olympian gods had finally come to an end with the defeat of the Titans. Zeus, leader of the gods, established his rule in heaven and imprisoned his enemies in Tartarus, a dark domain under the earth.

Not all the Titans had fought against the Olympians. One of those who had helped Zeus was Prometheus, on whom Zeus decided to bestow his favor.

"I have made men and women, three races of them," he told Prometheus. "They did not please me. One race did nothing but eat and drink; another planned only evil things; the third fought among themselves, had no reverence for the gods, and no respect for anything. Nevertheless, mankind should have one more chance, and this time it will be you, not I, who will make a new race. Make men and women out of clay, mix in any other element they may need, and let them work out their destiny. Use any material that is on earth. But one thing you must not do. You must not take anything from the heavens, nothing that belongs to the immortal gods. If you do, there will be a punishment too terrible to contemplate."

Prometheus obeyed. He scooped up some wet clay, and began to shape creatures resembling the gods. In their bodies he built characteristics of all the animals: the pride of the lion, the cleverness of the fox, the loyalty of the dog, the bravery of the bull. He gave them knowledge as well as instinct so they would know how to plow a field, plant seed, cultivate a crop, and reap a harvest. He taught them how to tame wild things, shear sheep, and milk cows. He

9

showed them how to make tools out of stone and how to make weapons to protect themselves from the horns of deer and other beasts. He instructed them how to exist in the wilderness, how to erect shelters and eventually, how to build houses.

But they were not happy. They shivered miserably through the winters; they sickened on uncooked food; they could not bake bread, bend cold iron, or melt metal. One thing was needed, and that one thing was forbidden: fire, the heavenly fire that belonged to the gods. For a while Prometheus hesitated. He remembered Zeus's threat and realized that anyone who took anything that belonged to the gods would suffer terribly. But men needed the gift of fire; they needed it not only for comfort but also for their future.

Prometheus knew what he had to do and how to do it. He took a long hollow reed, dried it, and filled the inside with pith. He walked in and out of Olympus; none of the gods noticed what he was doing. He touched the gods' hearth-fire with his reed that looked like a walking stick, and a spark from the hearth caught on the pith which burned slowly like the wick of a candle. He brought this from Olympus, lit the first flame on earth, and taught men how to kindle fire whenever it was needed for warmth or for work, for cooking food, shaping metal tools, or creating things of beauty.

When Zeus saw smoke arising, he was furious. He thundered at Prometheus. "I warned you!" he stormed. "Because you dared to bring the gods' fire down to the earthlings you love so much, you shall never leave the earth again. You shall be chained to a rock on the highest peak of the bleak Caucasus. There you shall lie exposed to the heavens you violated. You shall be burned by the rays of the fiery sun and frozen by the icy winds of winter. You shall lie there sleepless and helpless, for no power will come to free you and no creature will hear you. Every day an eagle will tear your flesh and feed upon your liver, and every night the wound will heal so that the eagle can prey upon you again and again."

Prometheus was bound, fettered to the rock with chains of iron and manacles of brass. Years passed, the tortures continued, and Prometheus bore the cruelty of Zeus. He never cried out his agony, nor did he regret what he had done. From time to time Zeus sent a messenger to urge Prometheus to repent. Prometheus refused. Then said the messenger, "Zeus knows that you have some secret knowledge about the fate of the gods. If you will disclose the secret, Zeus will set you free."

Prometheus knew that one day Zeus would be dethroned by a son of his own, just as Zeus had overthrown his father. Prometheus knew who the mother would be, and Zeus needed to know the name of the mortal woman so he could guard against her offspring. But Prometheus refused to talk. He remained inflexible, suffering indescribable pain rather than help a tyrant who would not help mankind.

Finally he was freed, not by Zeus, but by Herakles—the Romans called him Hercules—who shot the eagle and restored Prometheus to liberty. Then he went back to work among men.

It was Prometheus (according to the ancients) who gave man humanity. From the Firebringer, mankind inherited his forethought, his fearless spirit as a fighter against tyranny, his courage and, most of all, his compassion for all people everywhere.

PANDORA

...The Fateful Casket

 ROMETHEUS had thought about mankind with such sympathy that he had dared to steal the needed fire from Olympus, and for this he was grievously punished by Zeus. But the lord of Olympus did not think this cruelty was enough. Prometheus had a brother, Epimetheus, and though he was harmless and slow-witted, Zeus extended his displeasure to him. He did not punish Epimetheus as brutally as he had done his brother; he had a more subtle plan. It was a scheme which would not only affect Epimetheus but also the whole race of human beings whom Prometheus had dared to help and who were living happily and untroubled.

Zeus ordered Hephaestus, the smith and artisan of the gods, to make a woman out of the materials of earth. Hephaestus took some river clay that had flakes of gold in it and began to make a lovely girl. In with the clay he mixed the fragrance of a river rose, the sweetness of Hymettus honey, the smoothness of a silver dolphin, the voices of larks and lake-water, the color of sunrise on snow, the warmth of a sunny morning in May. Then he summoned the Four Winds to breathe life into the new creation. Finally he called upon the goddesses to complete the work and grant the glowing figure a touch of their own powers.

"Hephaestus has given her beauty," said Aphrodite, "but I shall make her more beautiful by adding the spark of love. It will shine in her eyes, and everyone that looks on her will be enchanted."

"I shall make her wise," said Athene. "She shall be able to choose between false and true, between what men value and what she must know is worthless."

"I shall make her a woman, a puzzle to every man," said Hera, the wife of Zeus. "I shall make her a real woman, for I shall give her the gift of curiosity."

Smiling, the goddesses adorned her, and when Zeus beheld her grace, her garland of gold, and the glory of her endowments, he was as charmed as though he had been a mortal. "We will call her Pandora," he said, "Pandora, the All-Gifted. She shall become the bride of Epimetheus. But she shall not go empty-handed. She shall bring with her a casket, a box of magic as her dowry. And Hermes, my messenger, shall conduct her to earth."

Epimetheus could not understand why the gods had become concerned about him. He was dazzled by Hermes, and it was some time before he could believe that the exquisite creature brought by the messenger god was meant for him. Even after Hermes departed in a flashing cloud and Pandora stood blushing beside him, he was perturbed. He remembered how often his brother Prometheus had warned him, "Do not trust the gods. And beware especially of Zeus and anything he may send you." However, when Pandora looked in his eyes and smiled, he was, as Aphrodite had predicted, enchanted and ensnared. Yet, even as he took her in his arms, he cautioned her.

"We have reason to fear the gods," said Epimetheus, "and also their gifts," he added, pointing to the casket.

"But this is my dowry," murmured Pandora. "Zeus himself filled it with magic as a present for us. See how beautifully it is carved and painted. Look at the silver hinges and the great gold clasp that fastens it."

"Keep it well fastened," said Epimetheus, "otherwise I shall never rest easy. I do not know what the casket may contain, and I do not want to know. Promise me one thing. Never open the box. It is, I grant, a beautiful thing, too beautiful to destroy, and we will keep it. But hide it. Put it not only out of your sight but out of your mind. Then we shall both be content."

Happy that she could keep her dowry, Pandora put it under the bed and turned to her husband with love. And so for a long time nothing disturbed their married life and their continual joy in each other.

But, though Pandora benefited from the goddesses' gifts of beauty and wisdom, the gift of Hera had not been given in vain. For quite a while, Pandora restrained her curiosity about the wonderful casket. But with the passing of time she could not help wondering what it might contain. After all, it was *her* dowry, and she had a right to see what the greatest of the gods had conferred upon her. Then, ashamed of her weakness, she put the idea from her, and thought only of her delight in her home with Epimetheus.

One day, however, the curiosity, so long stifled, overmastered her.

"I shall only lift the lid," she said to herself, "and snatch a moment's glimpse of what may be inside. No matter what I see, I won't touch a thing. Surely there can be no harm in that."

Anxiously, as though she were being watched, she tiptoed to her room. Gently getting down on her hands and knees, she drew the casket from under the bed. Half fearfully and half eagerly she lifted the lid. It was only a moment and the lid was up only an inch, but in that moment a swarm of horrible things flew out. They were noisome, abominably colored, and evil-looking, for they were the spirits of all that was evil, sad, and hurtful. They were War and Famine, Crime and Pestilence, Spite and Cruelty, Sickness and Malice, Envy, Woe, Wickedness, and all the other disasters let loose in the world.

Hearing Pandora's scream, Epimetheus rushed in. But it was too late. He and Pandora were set upon and stung, and the evil spirits flew off to attack the rest of mankind.

"It is all my fault," cried Pandora. "If I had thought more about your warning and less about my own desires, I could have controlled my curiosity."

"The fault is mine," said Epimetheus. "I should have burned the box." Then he added, for the poison of Malice was already taking effect, "After all, you are what you are—only a woman—and what else could one expect of a woman."

Disconsolate that she had brought so harmful a dower to Epimetheus as well as to all other men and women, Pandora wept. It was hours before she let her husband comfort her. Finally, after she grew quiet, they heard a faint sound inisde the box.

"Lift the lid again," said Epimetheus. "I think you have released the worst. Perhaps something else, something better, is still there."

He was right. At the bottom of the box was a quivering thing. Its body was small; its wings were frail; but there was a radiance about it. Somehow Pandora knew what it was, and she took it up, touched it carefully, and showed it to Epimetheus. "It is Hope," she said.

"Do you think it will live?" asked Epimetheus.

"Yes," answered Pandora. "I am sure it will. Somehow I know that it will outlive War and Sickness and all the other evils. And," she added, watching the shining thing rise and flutter about the room, "it will never leave us for long. Even if we lose sight of it, it will be there."

She was no longer downhearted as Hope spread its wings and went out into the world.

BELLEROPHON

... *The Winged Horse*

ELLEROPHON was one of the most beautiful and most unfortunate of Greek youths. It was his beauty that brought about the first of his misfortunes. A king's wife fell madly in love with him. She begged Bellerophon to return her love, to betray the king, and to run away with her. When he refused, her love became hate and she determined to ruin him utterly. She told her husband that Bellerophon had dared to make love to her and that, to avenge her honor, he must be killed.

The king was deeply troubled. Bellerophon had always served him loyally and well. He could not bring himself to execute one who had been not only faithful but was also beloved by the people. Yet he knew he had to comply with his wife's demand. He thought of a plan to rid himself of the responsibility by sending Bellerophon to another ruler, the king of Lycia.

"You will be my messenger," he told Bellerophon. "You will deliver this sealed letter, a message of state, and you will be rewarded."

The king of Lycia received Bellerophon with pleasure. A feast was arranged in his honor and, after the festivities, Bellerophon presented the message. When the king broke the seal he could not believe what was written. The letter contained only a single sentence: "See that the bearer of this is put to death."

The law of hospitality had established a bond between host and guest. At the same time, the message implied that Bellerophon must have committed a crime meriting death, and the king of Lycia could not ignore a request, actually an order, from a fellow king. After unhappy deliberation, he thought of a compromise. He could not kill his visitor in cold blood, but he would get rid of him just as effectually in another way.

"I have heard of your bravery as well as your loyalty," he said to Bellerophon. "You could show both to me if you would."

"Tell me what need be done," said Bellerophon, "and I will do it."

"You can help me and my people," said the king of Lycia, "if you would undertake to rid the country of its curse, the Chimaera. Seen from a distance it looks harmless enough, for though its size is gigantic, it has the body of a goat. On closer inspection the monster is revealed to have the head of a lion and the tail of a dragon. The lion's mouth spits flame and the dragon's tail spews a poisonous black smoke. Unconquerable on the earth, it can only be attacked from the air. And there is only one way of achieving that. That way is to be astride Pegasus who has never permitted anyone, god or man, to approach it, let alone mount its back."

"What is this Pegasus?" asked Bellerophon. "And where can it be found?"

"Pegasus is a horse, but like no horse that has ever been. It was born of the sea, it is whiter than the whitest sea-foam, and it has wings wider and more powerful than any eagle. Its favorite place is a spring called Hippocrene, literally the Horse's Fountain—they say that the spring first gushed forth when Pegasus' hoof struck the

earth. It is sacred to the Muses and those who drink of it are inspired. You will probably find Pegasus there."

It did not take Bellerophon long to find Hippocrene. Something seemed to guide him, and there, resting beside the spring, stood Pegasus. Bellerophon realized at once why the winged horse was the symbol of poetry, of all that rouses and soars and lifts the spirit of man. Its flowing white mane moved in the wind like the white-capped waves from which it came. Its neck seemed clothed in thunder, and its eyes were stars.

Bellerophon crept forward, but before he could touch it, Pegasus shied, spread its wings and, with a dazzling sweep, cleaved the sky. Bellerophon waited, hoping to see it descend like a meteor, but it did not return. Bellerophon sat up all night and, toward dawn, he fell asleep.

In his sleep he had a dream. The goddess Athene appeared holding a shining something in her hand.

"Sleep well, Bellerophon, but not too long," said the vision. "When you wake you will find this at your feet. It will serve you well."

Bellerophon woke at once. At his feet was a harness of gold, smoother yet stronger than any bit and bridle ever made. It was formed for the horse he had seen at the spring. Even as he stared at the glittering gift, Pegasus swooped down from the sky. As it bent over to drink, Bellerophon drew nearer. The glorious creature did not seem to mind; in fact it whinnied softly while Bellerophon gentled its sides. It bowed its neck as if inviting the bridle, and Bellerophon slipped the golden harness over its head. Then he leaped upon its back.

Happy though he was, Bellerophon was no happier than Pegasus. The winged horse neighed delightedly, outraced the wind, dived through the clouds, and skimmed the mountaintops until it came to the Chimaera's lair. Looking up, the monster saw something that threatened, and it prepared to annihilate whatever it was. Black fire belched from its mouth; black smoke spouted from its tail. Pegasus circled above, out of its reach, but near enough for Bellerophon to shoot arrow after arrow. Desperately the Chimaera leaped at its enemy and, as it exposed its flank, Bellerophon drove his spear through its chest. The monster sank to the ground, staining the earth with a pool of black blood.

Bellerophon did not bother to cut off the head and bring it back in triumph. He was satisfied with what he had done. He had proved himself a hero. He was proud—too proud—and pride was his undoing. He forgot about Athene and the golden gift. He let himself believe that he had slain the Chimaera without assistance and that he needed no help to accomplish other heroic deeds. He came to regard Pegasus as his exclusive property, his private horse. He continued to ride it all over the earth and through the skies.

Pegasus permitted this, until one day Bellerophon decided to ride up into Olympus and prance among the gods. Pegasus showed it disapproved by drooping its wings and refusing to go above the clouds. Bellerophon did something he had never done before. He dug his spurs savagely in the horse's ribs. Outraged, shaking with pain, Pegasus gave a wild snort and pitched Bellerophon off his back.

Somehow Bellerophon survived, but he was broken in spirit as well as body. He had not been killed by a king or a monster, but he had been destroyed by his own pride. He had not learned that "pride goeth before destruction and a haughty spirit before a fall."

PHAETHON

... *The Chariot of the Sun*

"**M**OTHER**,**" said young Phaethon, "the boys are always making fun of me. They do not believe me when I tell them I am the son of a god. How can I prove that I am?"

"It should not be difficult," said his mother, the nymph Clymene. "Go and ask him."

"But I have never seen him. Where can he be found?"

"He is the sun god," said Clymene, "and he spends most of his time in the land where the sun rises earliest. Seek him there."

Apollo's palace was a miracle of marble. Every inch of it was patterned in gold and set with precious stones. The ceilings were ivory, the doors were silver, the walls glowed with sapphires brighter than the bluest skies. There were great murals representing the four elements—fire, air, water, and earth—and everything that walked or swam or flew was depicted so realistically that it seemed to be alive. Apollo himself was enthroned in burning splendor. Around him were his attendants: the Years, the Months, the Days, and the Hours. Behind him stood the Seasons: Spring carrying a sprig of the first green leaves, Summer crowned with a garland of roses, Autumn with a basket of grapes, and Winter glittering with diamonds of frost.

Phaethon entered the hall but he could not look at the face of Apollo. The light blinded him. Lowering his eyes, he approached hesitantly, afraid to speak.

Apollo broke the silence. "What brings you here?" he asked.

"My shame," answered Phaethon. "All my schoolmates mock me. They say I pretend to be of heavenly origin, but that I am actually the son of a common peasant. I must know who my father really is."

"You are my son," said Apollo. "There can be no doubt about it. None. To prove it you can have anything you desire, even if it is something no mortal might ask."

"Thank you, my father," said Phaethon. "I will request what no mortal has ever asked. For one day let me drive your chariot of the sun."

Apollo was aghast. "I made a foolish promise," he said. "But you make a demand that is not only foolish but dangerous. You are young, you are half mortal, and you ask what even the gods would not ask. Only I am permitted to guide the fiery steeds through the air. Jupiter himself, whose arm flings thunderbolts and whose eyes flash lightnings, could not drive that flaming car. Ask something else."

"There is nothing else for me," said Phaethon. "Driving your chariot through the sky would show that I, too, can control the source of light and heat. It would prove that I am truly your son."

"But consider," said Apollo. "The path through the heavens is so steep that it dizzies the mind. The horses can barely climb it, and I myself am often loath to look down and see the earth spinning so far below me. The chariot sends down showers of sparks as it burns in the upper air. At the zenith of the sky I can scarcely stand straight, and the descent is worse. It plunges so swiftly and so sharply that Neptune, god of the waters, fears that some day I will fall into the sea."

Phaethon shook his head. "I must do once what my father does every day," he said.

"Listen," said Apollo, anxiously. "Even if I were to consent, how would you know what course to take? The heavens are full of perils not only because of the height but also because of the crowded constellations. The stars are treacherous. There is the Scorpion with its blazing claws and the Crab with its pincers of fire. There are the open-jawed Lion and Sagittarius, the Archer, shooting arrows. Choose something—anything—except this one thing. Do not urge me to do what will not bring you honor but destruction. Be my companion as well as my son. Stay here with me."

But Phaethon could not be persuaded. He insisted that Apollo keep his promise. Wearily, the god consented and led the way to the chariot of the sun.

Phaethon was dazzled. What he saw was a burst of the yellowest gold, a glowing scintillation, a sun at rest. Apollo raised a hand and the Hours approached. They harnessed the shining horses which pawed the ground with glistening hooves. Then Apollo anointed his son's face with a powerful lotion so that it could withstand the heat, and covered his head with sun-rays.

"My son," he said, "since you must fulfill your desire, do not be over eager. Pay more attention to the reins than to the whip. The horses are wild for action. Your trouble will not be making them go faster but holding them back. Do not take the straight road, although it seems the easiest, but follow a wide curve to the left. Avoid both the north and south poles. Do not fly too high or you will scorch the planets, and do not fly too low or you will set the world on fire. Above all, keep to the track the wheels have made."

Phaethon was too impatient to pay attention to his father's advice. He leaped into the chariot, seized the reins, and flicked them across the horses' backs. The horses gave an exultant neigh, dug their heels in the ground, and shot up into space.

For a few moments all went well. Then the horses sensed that their master was not guiding them. They reared and plunged, tossing the chariot about like a ship in stormy seas. Phaethon did not know where he was or what to do. He did not know whether to tighten or loosen the reins. Terrified, he lost control and clung helplessly to the vehicle as it swayed perilously from side to side. Freed from restraint, the horses left the traveled track and rushed aimlessly among the stars. The chariot was jolted among the constellations; it barely escaped the Scorpion's claws and almost collided with the Crab. Saved from being wrecked, the chariot veered about and rocketed downward through smoking clouds. As it descended, the oceans began to steam, rivers dried up, forests caught on fire, cities were set ablaze, great tracts of harvest land became desert where nothing would ever bloom again, the faces of Ethiopians turned black. Had the chariot reached the earth, the entire world would have been consumed.

It was Jupiter who saved the world. He flung a bolt of lightning at the hapless youth, and Phaethon, his hair aflame, fell like a shooting star into the sea. The horses, relieved of their burden, found their way to the accustomed course and brought the chariot back to Apollo.

Water nymphs recovered Phaethon's body and built a tomb on a rocky headland for Apollo's reckless son. It bore this inscription:

> Here, on this lonely promontory,
>   Lies one who flew too hotly and too high;
> Yet it is youth's imperishable glory
>   To dare and do and, if need be, to die.

ATALANTA

...The Fleet-Footed Runner

 ATURE could not decide whether to make Atalanta a boy or a girl, so Atalanta, a king's daughter, had something of the nature of both. She grew up more beautiful than most women and more athletic than most men. She was skilled in wrestling and unsurpassed in running; no one in all of Greece was as fleet-footed as she. Her father was proud of her, so proud that he became terribly possessive. The thought that some day she might marry and leave him was a continual torment. The more suitors she attracted, the more worried he became.

Finally he issued a proclamation to the effect that any suitor for the hand of Atalanta had to race with her, and anyone who lost the race would lose his head. In spite of the risk, suitors still persisted, for she was much desired because of her beauty and also because the man who married her would some day be king. Many came, attempted to outrun Atalanta, lost, and were put to death.

One day Milanion, a youth from another city, followed the crowd to the race course. Atalanta had not yet arrived, but he saw several young men preparing for the race. Someone told him the conditions of the contest.

"They are mad," he said. "Only a fool would risk his life for a girl —especially when there are plenty of girls to be had without running after them!"

Then he saw Atalanta. He was wonderstruck, overcome by her beauty. When she removed her outer garment and stood straight and slim in her short tunic she reminded him of Artemis, the swift and unattainable goddess. Breathing hard, he watched her run.

There was no chance of her being overtaken, for she scudded over the earth on feet that never seemed to touch the ground. It was no longer a girl whose hair streamed over bare shoulders, but a swallow in flight, a wave of the sea, an arrow from the bow. At the start, the youth who was competing with Atalanta appeared to be keeping pace with her, and Melanion was envious that anyone should be at her side. He clenched his fists, thinking, for a moment, the youth might win. But Atalanta was far ahead of him at the finish, and the hapless youth was led off to be killed.

Next morning Melanion presented himself to Atalanta. He was

young and handsome, her completely masculine counterpart, and Atalanta blushed and dropped her eyes when they met his.

"You are a stranger here," she said softly. "You came to watch the running?"

"I came to run," said Melanion. "I would race with you."

"That is a wild thought," said Atalanta. "Think of the other youths who have lost their lives. Think of the doom that awaits you. You are too young. Save yourself for other ventures or," she whispered, "for some girl who may love you."

"The other runners were laggards," said Melanion. "Besides, your beauty disturbed them. It disturbs me, too. But once we are at the starting point I will not look at you."

Atalanta blushed again. "So be it," she said.

That night Melanion offered a sacrifice to Aphrodite. "O goddess of love," he prayed, "it is you who have affected not only my heart but also my mind. It is you who have led me on to the last recklessness. It is you who must help me now."

A nebulous form rose before him, and a voice spoke out of the mist. "Do not worry, ardent one. Until now your Atalanta has been a devotee of Artemis, the virgin huntress. Now she thinks of Aphrodite when she thinks of you. Her new-found heart would have you win, but her long-trained feet will not permit it. They move independent of her will."

"Then there is no help for me?" asked Melanion.

"No worshiper of Aphrodite ever prayed for help in vain. Here are three golden apples from the Garden of the Hesperides which only I may pluck. Carry them in your tunic. When you come to race you will know how to use them."

The mist cleared and, seeing and hearing nothing, Melanion thought he had been dreaming. But at his feet were three apples of gold. He put them in his tunic.

The crowd was larger than ever. The runners crouched at the starting point. The trumpets blared, and the runners were off. For a minute or two they ran side by side, Atalanta's hair blowing across Melanion's face. It was as if she tried to slacken her speed, but her feet refused to obey her. She passed him and, though she looked back, the distance between them increased.

Suddenly Melanion knew what to do. He tossed one of the golden apples in front of her. Atalanta was an undefeated athlete but she was also a woman. She stooped to pick up the shining thing and tucked it in her bosom. Melanion caught up with her, but in the next instant she bounded away from him. Melanion took a second apple, threw it a little to the left, and Atalanta had to go out of her way to get it. This time he passed her, but, although he gained ground, Atalanta flashed by. The goal was near, and he had only one apple left. He was panting; his throat was burning dry; his legs seemed weighted.

"O goddess," he gasped, "do not desert me now! Give me strength!"

New vigor powered his arm. He threw the third apple, threw it far to the right. For a moment Atalanta ignored the glittering bait. Then she took the risk, swerved to the right, and recovered lost ground. But either Melanion had a burst of new energy or Aphrodite caused the apples to grow large and heavy as lead in Atalanta's bosom. In either case Melanion was an inch ahead of Atalanta when, fainting, he fell across the finishing line.

The crowd cheered. The trumpets blared louder than ever. The victor was crowned with a laurel wreath. And Atalanta looked strangely happy for a woman, and a champion, who had just been defeated.

JASON

... *The Golden Fleece*

ASON, the son of a Greek king whose throne had been stolen from him by his half-brother Pelias, had been secretly brought up by Cheiron, the Centaur. When Jason was twenty, Cheiron sent him out to claim his rights. Pelias received him politely and pretended to allow his claim.

"It is time you came back," said Pelias. "You are young; I am old. You are almost ready to govern the country. I said *almost,* for first there is something that must be done. Years ago I had a cousin who was threatened with death and was saved by a ram. It was a magical ram—its fleece was gold—and it carried my cousin to the island of Colchis. There the ram was sacrificed to the gods, and the golden fleece was nailed to a tree in the middle of a grove guarded by a dragon. I will resign the kingdom to you when you bring me the Golden Fleece."

Pelias smiled. This young upstart will never sit on my throne, he told himself. Then he said to Jason, "Take your time. I am not in a hurry."

But Jason did not wait. He built a ship with fifty oars and manned it with the foremost heroes. He called the ship *Argo;* those who sailed on it were the Argonauts. They steered a straight course for Colchis, but were forced to stop at a place called Lemnos.

Lemnos was governed by women who had been badly treated by men and at first refused to permit Jason to land. But they were so impressed by the sight of the heroes in their gleaming armor—the shields covered with glistening brass, the gold helmets crested with flowing horsehair dyed in many colors, the bronze swords and silver-studded belts—that they forgot about their hatred of men and

29

swarmed about them. They coaxed the Argonauts to spend a year on the island; Jason had to beat the men to make them sail on.

After leaving, they landed at the foot of an unknown promontory where they were made welcome by the king of the country. A banquet was spread in their honor; they were presented with fine raiment, corn and wine, and other gifts for the journey. But that night while everyone slept, they were attacked by a band of six-handed giants who thrashed about with huge trees for clubs. The place was in an uproar—the men struggled in a welter of blackness, for all the lamps had been overturned—and the east showed streaks of red before the marauders were slain. Not until then did the dazed adventurers straggle back to the *Argo*.

A great wind had sprung up, but though the sails were set, the ship did not move. The heroes strained their muscles at the oars, but the vessel would not budge. Then Jason spoke:

"A man can work against the wind, but no man can work against the will of the gods. The gods are speaking to us. Something is wrong; something happened last night of which we know nothing. We must go back and find out what it is."

It was full day when they came to the king's house and there, in the midst of blood-spattered corpses, was the king who had come to aid them and who, in the darkness, had been struck with one of their arrows. It was a time of weeping and mourning. The Argonauts laid the body on a bed of white linen, and, after burying the king, returned to the boat and cast off.

It was not until they reached the land of the blind prophet Phineus that Jason learned what had to be done before he could reach Colchis and the Golden Fleece. "After you leave here you will come to a narrow body of water," said Phineus. "Some say it stretches to the ends of the earth and empties into the dark unknown. You must pass through that difficult water and its even more difficult entrance. Countless ships have foundered and have been lost at that entrance. It is called the Clashing Rocks, and that is an exact description. There are two immense rocks, actually two cliffs, which move with the waves. Continually they clash and grind, part, and clash again. Anything that passes between them—a ship, a man, even a small bird—is ground to shreds. Nevertheless, there is a way to avoid being crushed. As your ship nears the cliffs, release a dove or some other bird. Watch closely, and you will see the rocks close upon it. The moment after, the rocks will part—and that is your chance. Have your men row with utmost power. Bend every back, never look behind, and you will go through before the rocks come together again."

"And should we be fortunate to come through," said Jason, "what then?"

"Then," said Phineus, "you must navigate to the east. Keep the shore always in sight, and you will come to a place where a broad river cuts through a forest and foams into the sea. That will be your first sight of Colchis."

"And then?" persisted Jason.

"This is as much as I am permitted to tell you," said Phineus. "But this I can add. Once you are in Colchis, someone will look after you. Trust her. I can say no more."

The next morning the Argonauts went forth. Alternately sailing and rowing, following Phineus' directions, they approached the Clashing Rocks. There they stopped rowing, and Jason let loose a dove. It flew between the cliffs which came together with a thundering crash that sent up torrents of roaring spray. But the flight of the dove was so swift it passed through unharmed except for the loss of a single tail-feather. Then, as the monstrous rocks recoiled and the backwash threatened to engulf the *Argo,* Jason gave the command to row. Fifty backs bent and a hundred arms put every ounce of pulling power into the fateful moment. The cliffs rushed together again. By a hair's breadth the ship came through the boiling current as the rocks, meeting in a titanic collision, smashed and merged into one.

Stopping only at the first islet to give thanks to the gods and to swear never to desert each other no matter what might happen, the heroes sailed for many wearying days, passing many strange places, before they came to the island of the brazen birds. The birds were literally brazen for their beaks and claws and even their feathers were brass. Moreover, the birds could shoot their feathers with arrow-like precision, and the Argonauts had to keep their helmets on to ward off those deadly feathers. They stayed only long enough to supply themselves with provisions and fresh water. Then, sailing along a broad river that cut through a forest, they arrived at Colchis. There they held a council.

"Before we attempt to take the Golden Fleece by force, let us try persuasion," said Jason. "Soft words are sometimes better than hard blows. Perhaps the ruler of the country will present us with the fleece either as a favor or because of our rightful claim. Carry your swords, but keep them sheathed as we approach."

The king's palace was a marvel. Before it stood a fountain from which issued four streams. The first was perfume, the second milk, the third wine, and the fourth water which was pleasantly warm in winter and sparkling cold in summer. The sides of the palace were carved and crowned with fantastic figures. They were embellished with bronze ornaments and sparkled with designs of colored stones. The roof was burnished copper. The king himself was even more imposing; he outshone his surroundings. In the morning light he gleamed like the sun itself. But there was no warmth in his expression as he addressed the Argonauts.

"What have you come to steal?" he said sternly. "The Greeks are notoriously great robbers, and I know what to expect. But we of Colchis also know how to take care of ourselves and our possessions. You are a scant fifty; we have thousands in arms. Beware before you begin plundering."

Some of the heroes angrily put their hands on their swords, but Jason answered without raising his voice. "We have come on a peaceful mission, O king. We seek neither spoils nor slaves. We have come to offer our services for a small return."

"And what may that be?" asked the king coldly.

"I will put my men—all champions—at your disposal. We will help you clear the borders of Colchis of all opposing forces. We will join you to subdue your enemies and humble your foes. In return we ask something which has no value except to me."

"And that is?" sneered the king.

"The Golden Fleece," said Jason.

"You are mad," said the king contemptuously, "and it is forbidden to kill madmen. You are also arrogant, and in Colchis we cut out the tongues of boasters. Since you are armed, look to your arms."

But there was no bloodshed. At that moment the king's daughter, Medea, came through the palace doors. She had the gift of magic and it had been revealed to her that she would fall in love with a hero from across the dark sea. She stood there gazing at Jason and knew that this was the man. Jason, too, knew that something fateful was about to happen to him.

"O king," said Jason with his eyes on Medea. "It is true that we are armed. Nevertheless, we are men of peace. Fate has brought us here. We would be your supporters, not your usurpers. Propose a test, and we will fulfill it. Show us your favor, and we will be worthy of your trust."

Jason's courteous answer calmed the king. He was also aware that his daughter was looking at the dauntless hero as she had never looked at a man before.

"You are our guests," said the king. "One does not quarrel with one's guests but invites them to share whatever one's house may have to offer. Let us go inside."

After the dinner had been eaten and the court poet had sung in praise of his master's deeds of valor and the wine cups were lifted in toasts of mutual regard, the king spoke to Jason.

"I repent of my hasty words. I should not have doubted your peaceful intentions. Since you have come in peace to fulfill a vow, I will let you have the Golden Fleece. But, since you are heroes, you will, I know, want to prove yourselves. That is altogether proper. So, as you requested, I shall propose a test. I have two brazen-footed bulls who breathe fire. You must yoke these oxen and plow four acres with them in the field of Ares. Then you are to sow the furrows, not with seed but with dragon's teeth. From the teeth there will spring up a crop of fierce soldiers. After you have yoked the bulls and plowed the fields and sowed the dragon's teeth *and* overcome the army that will arise, you may take the Golden Fleece."

For a moment Jason was speechless. Then, without a quiver in his voice, he replied: "You are the ruler here. You make the rules, and you have the right to propose the tests. I cannot tell how I am to go about such impossible tasks, but I shall try. It was destined that I come here. If I am to die that is part of my destiny."

That night Medea secretly came to Jason and, blushing, she said: "You will think me shameless. It is not maidenly to confess love without waiting to be asked. Nor should a king's daughter declare herself to a stranger. But there is nothing else I can do—I am moved by too great a passion and I must cast modesty aside. There is another reason for this midnight visit. Though you have not appealed to anyone for aid, I am here to help you."

"You?" said Jason incredulously.

"I am a niece of Circe the enchantress. Her blood is in my veins and her art is in my brain. I know you are without fear, but I also know that you will die tomorrow unless you heed me tonight."

"What am I to do?" asked Jason.

"Listen," whispered Medea. "Here is a box of ointment. It was made from the root of a flower which sprang from the blood of Prometheus as he lay in agony on his ice-cold rock. Spread this over

your body and fire will not touch you. Anoint your shield with it and no spear will be able to pierce it. Run it along your sword and it will never break."

"And what can I do in return for such unlooked-for protection?" said Jason, adding quickly, "and such loving care?"

"Take me with you when you go," urged Medea. "Take me wherever you are going."

"You shall come with me to Thessaly," said Jason. "And when I am enthroned you shall be my queen." And he kissed Medea.

In the morning the king and his court were waiting for him. "Jason," said the king, "here is a helmet full of dragon's teeth. However, before you sow them, you must catch my fire-breathing bulls, harness them both to the yoke, and plow four acres no matter what happens We will watch," he added grimly, "while you go to the field of Ares, the war god."

As soon as Jason reached the field a gate was opened, and the bulls leaped out. Pawing the ground with their hooves of brass, they rushed at Jason; fire came from their mouths and poisonous smoke poured from their nostrils. Sheets of flame swept around Jason, but he never stepped aside. Instead, he caught one bull by the horn and, forcing it to its knees, dragged it to the yoke. Waves of fire and smoke continued to gush from the other bull, but Jason was prepared. He struck at its legs, forced it down, and fastened both bulls to the yoke with the bronze plow behind them. Then, using his spear as a goad, he drove the bellowing animals, still spouting flame, before him, making deep ruts in the ground and dropping the dragon's teeth from the helmet in the furrows.

Scarcely had he finished his plowing when the earth began to heave, and out of every furrow sprang armed men. They advanced against Jason. But Jason was prepared. He threw the empty helmet among them, and the men began to fight for it. Furiously they fought, one against the other, until not one was left alive, and the earth that had borne them took them back again.

"I have done what was demanded," Jason told the king. "Now give us the Golden Fleece."

"I never said I would *give* it to you," said the king blandly. "I said that, after you had performed the tasks, you could *take* it. Take it, then. Go to the grove where the fleece hangs on a certain tree. You will find the grove easily, for it is guarded by a dragon as long as your ship. The dragon has a thousand coils; its scales are metal; its claws are pointed steel. It cannot be killed. Perhaps the dragon will let you take what you want. Go ahead. Try to take it."

It was dark when Jason came to the woods. He was not alone. Medea was with him and she spoke. "My father does not expect you to come back. He knows no force can conquer the immortal monster. He plans to burn your ship and destroy your companions."

"Why, then, did you come with me?" asked Jason. "To see me die?"

"To keep you alive," answered Medea.

"But if the dragon cannot be slain how can it be subdued?" asked Jason.

"By a spell," answered Medea. "You shall see."

When it heard the mortals coming, the dragon lifted its enormous head, thrashed its killing tail, roared louder than a herd of bulls, and belched flames higher than the trees. But Jason and Medea kept their distance and waited until it grew calm. Then

Medea began singing, a tender, lulling song that had soothed children since the beginning of time. The dragon listened, then it licked her hand, then it nodded, and then it fell asleep.

Stroking the great beast's head with one hand and clasping Jason's arm with the other, Medea guided her lover through the heart of the grove to the dark tree that held the Golden Fleece. Carefully Jason took down the coveted treasure, and the two sped down to the beach where the ship was moored. There was great joy but little time for rejoicing as Jason and Medea came aboard and the *Argo* fled hurriedly into the west.

The voyage back was long and full of troubles. The king of Colchis sent a fleet to capture Jason and the Argonauts, and Medea's brother, who commanded one of the ships, was killed. Storm after storm pounded the vessels. Sirens tried to entice the men to change their course; monsters threatened to seize them. Finally the Argonauts reached the homeland and Jason presented the Golden Fleece to Pelias. But Pelias refused to surrender the throne. Never expecting Jason to return, he had killed Jason's parents so that he could rule unchallenged. Again Medea used her magic, and by it Pelias lost his life.

Jason was now lord of Thessaly and, until an unforeseen fate overtook him, he and Medea, now man and wife, lived quietly. He had seen enough bloodshed and needed no new adventures. He liked to wear the simple attire of a countryman, but his cloak was lined with a fleece of gold.

ARACHNE

...*The Eternal Spinner*

RACHNE was a Lydian princess, but she was prouder of her skill than of her ancestry. Lydia was famous for its brilliant dyes, and Arachne used them in the threads she spun and the cloths she wove so wonderfully. When she sat plying her shuttle there were always onlookers exclaiming: "What loveliness!" "Such delicate details!" "Athene herself, goddess of all household arts, could not do better!"

One day an old woman stood among the admiring group. "You weave well," she said. "It is almost as though you had been instructed by the goddess Athene herself."

"Thank you," replied Arachne, "but I need no instruction from anyone. I taught myself."

"Be careful," warned the old woman. "Do not boast. Athene might hear you. Her woven work is admired by all the gods."

"I do not care," said Arachne petulantly. "I am not afraid of her. If Athene were to appear this moment, I would dare her to match my spinning and weaving."

At that instant a change came over the old woman. Her gray hair turned to gold, her rags fell off, revealing the white robe of the severest goddess, and on her head was the shining helmet of Athene. "I accept the challenge," she said.

Arachne grew pale, but she was not daunted. "There is another spindle," she said, pointing to the opposite window. "I presume you have brought your own wool."

"You are impertinent," said Athene. "But as the challenger you have the right to choose a subject for the contest."

"Very well, I will," said Arachne unabashed. "Since my rival is an immortal, let us see who can most successfully depict the adventures of the gods and goddesses."

Athene began, but everyone watched Arachne. It was not only what she did but how she did it. She took up the yarns of wool with the lightest of hands, separated the strands till they were barely visible threads of white and pink, yellow and green, purple and gold. Then, selecting one color after another, she carded the material, twirled the spindle, and passed the shuttle in and out among the interlacing yarns. Warp and woof threads soon formed a web, and the web developed into a growing pattern marvelous to behold.

Athene's fingers flew fast. She had decided to portray one of her own exploits, her contest with Poseidon for the land of Attica. One could see the great sea god in all his vibrant power, striking the ground with his trident, forcing up a gushing spring; while Athene was producing an olive tree, which had been judged the more useful gift and had caused the city of Athens to be named in her honor.

Arachne's fingers were not faster, but her work was far more startling. With supreme impudence she depicted the lawless love affairs of Athene's father, the great Zeus himself. She showed Zeus disguised as a swan and caressed by Leda; Zeus as a bull carrying off Europa on his back; Zeus in a shower of gold entering the tower in which Danae's father had imprisoned her; Zeus showing himself to Semele in a fatal flash of lightning.

The onlookers were amazed. They were frightened when they saw the expression on Athene's face. The goddess could not deny the beauty of Arachne's workmanship, but she was outraged by the insolence of her mortal rival, and even more by the feeling that, for all her craft, she had been surpassed. Without a word she tore the web from Arachne's hands and destroyed it. Then she touched Arachne's forehead. Terrified by Athene's wrath and cursed by the goddess' touch, Arachne lost her reason. Overcome by shame and guilt, she ran from the room. Outside she found a rope and hanged herself.

When Athene saw the poor girl dangling in mid-air, she said, "You will not die, but that is how you will live. You will be shrunken and you will be feared. You will hang suspended much of the time from a thread, and, since you are such a spinner, you will spin forever, spinning one web after another until the end of time."

So it came to pass. The object of Athene's jealousy is still to be seen. In every cobweb, spinning her thread, or descending from it, she lives. The naturalists know her by her name: the spider is called Arachne.

PYGMALION

... *The Marvelous Statue*

YGMALION was a famous sculptor born on the island of Cyprus. A woman had hurt his pride when he was very young and he had turned his back on love. He shunned the society of all men and women, content to live alone, surrounded by the marble images he carved. He convinced himself that his statues were not only more pleasing to look at but also better company than people.

One day he finished a statue that surpassed anything he had ever attempted. It was the ideal figure of a beautiful woman. Instead of using marble, Pygmalion had made it out of ivory, and the texture was so delicate that it seemed to glow. Something happened to Pygmalion that he had not foreseen. He fell in love with his own creation. Bewildered, he prayed to Aphrodite.

"O goddess," he implored. "Forgive me. I have neglected you shamefully for years. Now I see my folly. If I could only find a woman as lovely as this image, I would humbly ask her to be my wife, and both of us would worship at your shrine."

He heard or thought he heard a voice, Aphrodite's voice, saying, "Observe your handiwork more closely."

When Pygmalion looked at the statue again the glow seemed to have increased. The ivory had taken on a rosy tint; the cold chiseled surface seemed to have grown soft and warm. His pulse beat fast. If only the thing he had made could feel his passion! If only his prayer could be answered!

"There stands your answer," said a voice. "Take her in your arms."

Pygmalion did not hesitate. He clasped the statue and found it flesh. He kissed it, and his kisses were ardently returned. The image he had created had come marvelously alive.

"Oh, Aphrodite," exclaimed Pygmalion, "you are truly the goddess of love! You have warmed the marble into a woman and given me a wife. I will call her Galatea."

ENDYMION

... The Sleeping Shepherd

A thing of beauty is a joy for ever:
Its loveliness increases. It will never
Pass into nothingness, but will still keep
A bower quiet for us, and a sleep
Full of sweet dreams, and health, and quiet breathing.

HIS IS how Keats begins his long poem "Endymion," the very music of whose name went into the poet's being.

Endymion was a shepherd whose beauty was so great that even the immortals on Olympus envied him. Diana, the chaste moon goddess, went further: she fell in love with him. Hers was a love that was not only passionate but also possessive. Usually cold hearted, her whole nature changed when she saw Endymion lying on the mountainside gazing dreamily at the moon. Clothed in moonbeams, Diana came down to earth and ardently kissed him while he slept.

Endymion felt the warmth of that kiss quicken his blood, but when he woke he saw nothing. Diana had vanished.

"Dear goddess," he prayed, "if it was nothing but a dream, let me dream forever. Let me never wake, but let me slumber on throughout eternity."

Diana was glad to grant his wish. Endymion would be hers forever, hers alone. Holding him in a perpetual sleep, she kept him from all others, entered his dreams, and covered him with kisses. Night after night she visited him. Night after night she lulled him in moonlight, a bower of serenity, "and a sleep full of sweet dreams."

42

NARCISSUS AND ECHO

...*Their Hopeless Love*

ON OF a blue-eyed nymph, Narcissus inherited his mother's ravishing beauty. He did not realize how beautiful he was, for he had never seen his image in a mirror or reflected in a pool. At his birth it had been foretold that Narcissus would lead a happy life if, the oracle warned, "he never sees himself as he is." This made little sense to his mother, who promptly forgot about it. Nor did it worry Narcissus. No one had ever repeated the prophecy to him.

The boy grew up, wandering in the fields, teasing the forest animals, and playing by himself. He did not want companions; he was happiest when he was alone. The truth is that he was indifferent to others, for his heart was too cold to care for anyone. This did not prevent others from falling in love with him and being broken-hearted when their love was not returned.

The one who loved him most passionately—and most hopelessly—was the nymph Echo. Echo had been one of Hera's handmaidens, but she had incurred the goddess' displeasure because of her wagging tongue. A constant chatterer, Echo could not resist spreading gossip and repeating the smallest bit of scandal. Once, when Zeus was enjoying himself with some of the mischievous mountain nymphs, Echo kept telling stories so that her jealous mistress' attention was diverted from her husband's behavior.

"This is too much!" said the imperious Hera to Echo when she realized what had happened. "You are dismissed from our court. Your tongue is far too loose, you love to chatter, and chatter you shall. But the chatter will not be your own. You shall keep on repeating everything you hear. That will be all you can say. You shall never speak first. You have always wanted to have the last word. Well, you shall have it—but that is *all* you shall have."

Sadly Echo followed Narcissus wherever he went. She knew he had rejected love, so she walked stealthily for fear of being repulsed. "If only I could talk, I would woo him," she thought. "I could teach him the language of love, and I would win him. But, alas, I can say nothing by myself; I can only answer. And he will never speak to me." Her mind was so full of grief that one day she grew careless and, in her haste to catch up with him, she stumbled over some dry branches.

Narcissus was startled by the sound. He could not tell whether it was a wild animal or some hunter who had lost his way. He shouted, "Is anyone here?"

"Here," replied Echo softly.

"I cannot see you," said Narcissus. "Reveal yourself! Come!"

"Come!" Echo answered.

"Where are you?" continued Narcissus. "What do you want if I can find you?"

"You!" Echo repeated.

"This is a silly game," grumbled Narcissus impatiently. "Let me see you. Let us get together."

"Together!" cried Echo joyfully, as wild with eagerness, she disclosed herself. She ran through the bushes and threw her arms about his neck. But Narcissus pushed her away. "Begone!" he shouted roughly. "I will die before I let you have me!"

"Have me!" urged Echo tearfully.

Narcissus shook her off and vanished through the trees, leaving Echo to mourn and pine. She haunted lonely glens and hidden caves. Her limbs shrank with longing, her body wasted away, until all that was left was her voice, a thin little voice that still answers when someone calls.

Meanwhile, running away from Echo, Narcissus had come upon a pool. Fed by a crystal spring, unsullied by passing cattle or even a dead leaf, it was shaded from the sun and bordered with a cool bed of mint and sweet-smelling grasses. Bending down to drink, Narcissus saw his reflection in the mirror-clear water. Never had he seen anything so beautiful. For the first time in his life, he fell in love. He did not know that the blue-eyed youth was himself, and when his lips met his own lips he tried to embrace the image that

melted in his grasp. The wonderful face in the water wavered and seemed to mock him.

"If," he complained, "this is what love is, it is an agony. I know what others must have suffered when they could not gain the object of their desire. Therefore," he said to his image, "do not avoid me. Many have yearned for me, but I have disdained them all. I have kept my love for you, you only." He wept, and as his tears fell into the pool the water rippled and the image was shattered.

Hour after hour and day after day Narcissus lay beside the pool, looking disconsolately at his reflection and begging it to respond. He could not break the spell of self-enchantment; he could neither capture nor give up the beloved image. "Alas," he grieved. And Echo answered, "Alas!"

Enraptured, like Echo, he languished and faded away. The rosy flesh lost its color; his ivory-white body sank into the earth.

It was the earth which revived his beauty. Early the following year, in the very spot where he had died, there rose a flower unsurpassed in grace and cool perfection. It was a pure white narcissus.

IPHIGENIA

... The Transported Sacrifice

HE Greek fleet, numbering more than a thousand ships equipped for a long war against Troy, lay becalmed at Aulis. Days went by, but there was no sign of a breeze; the warriors fretted while the vessels remained weather bound. It was, all Artemis' doing. Agamemnon of Mycenae, leader of the Greeks, had offended the goddess by shooting a female deer sacred to her. Agamemnon consulted the expedition's priest and prophet.

After performing the required ceremonies, the priest left the altar and inquired what Agamemnon valued most.

"Nothing is dearer to me than my daughter, Iphigenia. I value her more than I do my own life," he said.

"Then," said the priest, "that is what you must sacrifice. If you do that, the goddess will forgive you, a strong wind will spring up, and the Greeks will be on their way to conquer Troy."

Agamemnon was appalled. "I cannot do it. It is too much even for a deity to ask. Rather than cause the death of my own child I will resign my command."

The Greeks would not hear of Agamemnon's relinquishing the leadership. They threatened to revolt. They argued that, heartless as it seemed, the loss of a girl, even a cherished daughter, was little compared to the loss of an entire army. The war, they insisted, had to be won, and at any cost. Agamemnon finally yielded. He schemed to make the blow less terrible to his family. He sent a message to his wife that a marriage had been arranged with the hero Achilles, and that Iphigenia, dressed in bridal attire, should be brought to Aulis.

When she arrived. Iphigenia threw her arms about her father. "How good it is to be with you again," she cried. "But why do you look so sad? Never mind. Those lines will soon vanish from your forehead now that we are once more together. We must make a thanksgiving sacrifice."

Agamemnon shuddered. The word sacrifice chilled his bones. He turned away.

Meanwhile Agamemnon's wife had met Achilles and spoke rapturously of the coming wedding.

"What wedding?" asked Achilles. "Surely you cannot mean that I am to be the bridegroom. Your daughter is a lovely girl, but I never saw her until today. I assumed she had come to be with her father before we sail—if we ever get a wind."

Agamemnon was forced to tell the truth. He stammered, faltered, and found it difficult to speak, but he had to confess the terrible thing that had to be done. No one had a word to say in his behalf, no one except Iphigenia.

"If it is my lot to be sacrificed for a cause, I offer my life willingly," she said calmly. "I am here, dressed for a wedding, though my bridegroom is Death. When my countrymen win the war, the victory will not only be theirs, it will also be mine. My throat is bared for the knife. I am ready."

The knife never reached her throat. As the blade descended, Iphigenia was no longer there. In her place stood a female deer, the very one that Agamemnon had shot.

"A miracle!" exclaimed the priest. "The girl's great courage has won the favor of Artemis. The goddess has forgiven her father."

The last words were lost in a rush of wind. Everyone looked toward the harbor. Waves were gathering force and the sails of the ships were straining to be at sea. There was no trace of Iphigenia. She had been transported by Artemis to Tauris, to serve as priestess in the temple of the goddess.

The Taurians were a savage and suspicious lot. They demanded that any stranger who landed on their shores had to be sacrificed. Iphigenia did not have to do the actual killing, but she had to consecrate and prepare the victims for death. Remembering what had almost happened to her in Aulis, she wept every time a stranger set foot in Tauris.

For several years she had been serving what she considered a murderous priesthood when news was brought to her that a Greek ship had anchored in the harbor. The two young men who came from the vessel claimed that it had been driven to the shore by a storm, but this was not the case. Orestes, Iphigenia's brother, and

his friend Pylades had sailed it to Tauris for a particular purpose. Orestes had committed a crime, and the only way he could atone for it would be by taking the statue of Artemis away from the brutal Taurians and bringing it, unsullied, to Athens. The Furies had driven Orestes temporarily mad, and he was so marked by grief that, when he was brought to the temple, Iphigenia did not recognize him.

The years had changed Iphigenia, too; Orestes was a child when he had last seen her. He remembered his sister only vaguely. She only knew that both strangers were Greek and that she had to consecrate them for the sacrifice. Horrified, as always, at the thought of bloodshed and full of compassion for the young men, she questioned Orestes.

"Where are you from, and what is your name?"

"I am an exile from Mycenae. I have no name."

"Mycenae!" exclaimed Iphigenia. "Mycenae where Agamemnon is king?"

"Where Agamemnon *was* king," said Orestes grimly. "Ask me no more."

"But I must know," insisted Iphigenia. "How did he die? Was he slain? If so, by whom?"

"His wife was faithless," said Orestes bitterly. "She conspired with her lover. Then she killed her husband. That is how Agamemnon was murdered."

"And she—his wife—is living?"

"No," replied Orestes. "Her son killed her. It was a ghastly crime. But his father had to be avenged."

"And his sister—the one they call Iphigenia—where is she?"

"I do not know," said Orestes. "I only know she, too, is dead."

There was a long silence. Then Iphigenia spoke again.

"If," she said slowly, "instead of preparing both of you for the sacrifice, I were to set you free, would you carry me away from these hateful people and this hideous task? Would you take me to Mycenae?"

"Why Mycenae?" asked Pylades.

"Because I want to find wherever my brother may be. I want to tell him that his sister Iphigenia has never stopped hoping to be reunited with him."

"You must be mad!" shouted Orestes. "How can you know what Iphigenia ever hoped! Enough of this! Iphigenia is dead. I am her brother, Orestes."

"Then both of us are mad, for it is your sister Iphigenia who speaks. If we are mad, it is a wonderful madness! After so many years of misery so much happiness!" She clasped him passionately. Suddenly her face clouded. "But what made you come here?"

"To atone for my sin I must bring the statue of Artemis to Athens," said Orestes. "Or die."

"You shall not die," said Iphigenia. "I have thought of a way to save us. I shall say that you, a madman, dared to touch the sacred statue and because of that touch the statue has been defiled. To remove the taint I must take the image to the sea and there cleanse the statue in salt water. I shall say that the strangers must also be purified before they can be sacrificed."

The Taurians were crowded around the temple waiting for the bloody sacrifices. When Iphigenia, holding the statue of the goddess in her arms, told them about the "madmen," they were suspicious and fearful. They drew back. With slow steps, in solemn dignity, Iphigenia, Orestes, and Pylades walked to the shore. The people muttered, fearing a trick but, unwilling to touch a madman, allowed them to pass.

The priests, realizing the truth, rallied the Taurians to attack and seize the deceivers. But it was too late. Orestes' ship, unmoored, was safely on its way to Mycenae.

AENEAS

...His Wanderings

HE GREEKS had won. Troy was in flames; its once topless towers lay in ruins; those of its people who had not died were fleeing the city. Aeneas was one of those who escaped. Carrying his aged father, Anchises, on his shoulders, Aeneas set out with other refugees to find a place to live. He had no idea where it would be, but it seemed to him that destiny pointed to the west. For a while Aeneas and his Trojan followers stayed near the sea. Finally, they built ships and started on their long voyage.

It was on the island of Delos that Aeneas received assurance that they were headed in the right direction. "Seek your ancient mother," the oracle told him. "Your true home is far; it is in the place from which your race first sprang. There you shall dwell and there you shall rule." It was a hopeful but puzzling prediction.

"I seem to remember a legend about our ancestors," said old Anchises. "I was told that they came from Crete." Since Crete was not far from Delos, everyone looked forward to an early end of travel and a permanent home.

Unfortunately the settlement on Crete was a disaster. The land was bleak, the soil was stubborn, the crops failed. Worse, pestilence broke out and took the lives of many. It was apparent that Crete was not to be a homeland. A dream confirmed Aeneas' suspicion that they had come to the wrong place.

"Your destined place is not here," said a figure in his dream, "but much farther west. The cradle of your race is Hesperia, to be known as Italy. There a nation will be built."

Once more Aeneas and his group embarked, and once more they encountered trouble. A storm drove them to a coast occupied by the

Harpies, weird half-human creatures, huge birds of prey whose upper half was the body of a woman. As soon as the Trojans had landed and had brought out food, the Harpies swooped down, seized whatever they fancied, and covered the rest with filth. It was impossible to catch the creatures which flew faster than any arrow and which, since their appetites were never satisfied, filled the air with long and hideous screams. This was no place to live. Aeneas set out again.

It was a hazardous journey. Aeneas had to avoid not only the difficult passages, such as the straits of Scylla and Charybdis, where Odysseus had lost six of his men, but all cities occupied by the Greeks. Taking the long way, Aeneas plotted his course carefully and was rounding the island of Sicily when a storm worse than any he had ever experienced hit him. Violent gales tossed the ships about as though they were toys. The waves seemed high enough to wash the stars and the spaces between them so deep that the sailors thought they could see the bed of the ocean. Fortunately none of the ships capsized. Though badly battered, they rode out the tempest and, one by one, reached land. They had come to Carthage.

Carthage was a noble city on the coast of Africa. Its ruler was the rich and beautiful Dido, whose husband had been killed and who had vowed never to marry again. Aphrodite, the love goddess, had been unable to make Dido change her mind, but when Aeneas stood on the coast, wondering where he was, Aphrodite determined to bring the young wanderer and the lovely widow together.

Dido welcomed Aeneas graciously. "As one who has suffered," she said, "I have learned to help others who have been unfortunate." She entertained the Trojans with unstinting hospitality, honored

them at banquets, and arranged games for them and her own countrymen. After the festivities, she persuaded Aeneas to tell his story.

Happy to have so splendid and sympathetic a listener, Aeneas
related what had happened since the fall of Troy. He told how, after
a bitter siege, the Greeks had entered the city by a paltry trick, how
the Trojans had been betrayed, how the priest Laocoon had been
killed for daring to warn the inhabitants of Troy, how the town had
been destroyed, and how, although he managed to escape, his wife
had been lost in the flight.

Listening to Aeneas' recital, Dido fell in love with him. She confessed it.

"I have sworn never to remarry," she said. "But there is a bond
between us stronger than a vow. You have lost a wife; I have lost a
husband. Fate has cast you on these shores; fate has brought us
together. End your wanderings here."

For a while this seemed the ideal solution. Dido was entranced
with her hero; he was captivated by his lovely admirer. She arranged
hunting expeditions and other parties for him; she planned special
diversions for his companions; she never tired of listening to the
story of his adventures. As her devotion grew more and more grati-
fying, the idea of leaving this perfect situation for some vague future
seemed less and less desirable.

Nevertheless, Aeneas was troubled. He began to have bad dreams,
dreams that reminded him of his mission, dreams in which he was
punished for idling away his time. Again and again a shrouded figure
appeared in a dream to reproach him.

"You are escaping again," it said in the voice of the oracle. "But
this time you are deceiving yourself. You are trying to escape your
destiny. Your destiny is not here but where you must build a nation.
It is not Carthage but Hesperia. Rouse yourself. Seek your rightful
place."

Dido was distracted when Aeneas told her he must resume his
wandering. "How can you think of leaving me!" she wept, throwing
herself in his arms. "Carthage is yours, as I am. I have asked nothing
of you except to share my love and my delight. This is your home.
Have you grown tired of it—or me?"

Aeneas assured her that he would never cease loving her but,
although he was grateful for all she had done, he could not stay. "It
is my destiny," he said.

"Your destiny!" she cried scornfully, and flung herself away from
him. All through the preparations for Aeneas' departure, she told

herself he would change his mind. She hid herself, hoping that he would need her and hold her again in his arms. But the preparations went on. Aeneas came to bid good-by, but she would not speak to him. There was still the possibility that he would relent and stay. It was only when she saw the fleet sailing away that she broke down. The blow to her pride as well as to her love was greater than she could bear. Looking back at Carthage, Aeneas saw flames rising from its center. He did not know that Dido had ordered the erection of a pyre, that she had lit the funeral pile and had cast herself upon it.

There was no rejoicing when the Trojans finally landed on the Italian shore. Aeneas' father had died during the journey and the chief pilot, Palinurus, had been drowned. Aeneas went at once to the cave of the Cumean Sibyl, the prophetess who could foresee his future. After performing the required rites, she spoke.

"You will face new troubles, but you will not be defeated by them. Every disaster will make you press on with more determination."

"But what troubles? What disasters?" asked Aeneas. "When will it all end?"

"Such questions cannot be answered here," replied the Sibyl. "The answers lie in another world. First you must try the regions beneath the earth. The descent is easy; the way back is hard. I will guide you and we will take with us a golden branch as a talisman. You will see sights to make anyone quail. You will need all your courage. Follow me."

It was a dark and hideous region that they entered. Weird specters and ghostly monsters appeared everywhere. Aeneas came face to face with the lion-dragon Chimaera armed with flame. He was challenged by the hundred-handed Briareus with a sword in every hand. He stared at the many-headed Hydra hissing from all its snake-like mouths. Aeneas would have fought with them, but the Sibyl reminded him that they were all unreal, disembodied spirits of things that once created terror but could no longer harm.

Pressing on, Aeneas and the Sibyl came to a river whose banks were thick with jostling crowds trying to get into a small boat. The ferryman took some aboard but pushed others rudely back.

"Why are some favored," asked Aeneas, "and not others?"

"This is the river Styx, the river of the Underworld, and the ferryman is Charon who takes on board only those who have had proper burial," replied the Sibyl. "The others, the unburied dead, must wander for a hundred years before they can rest here."

In the crowd Aeneas recognized Palinurus, the pilot who had been swept overboard in the storm, and grieved for him.

"He will not have to suffer long," said the Sibyl. "The people who found his body will see that it is buried with all due ceremonies. Bid him farewell, for the boat is full and Charon cannot wait."

At first Charon refused to take Aeneas, a living man, but the Sibyl waved the golden branch and they were brought to the opposite shore. As they disembarked, all three of Cerberus' heads growled and showed their teeth. But the Sibyl threw it a honey-cake, and the watchdog of Hades allowed them to pass on.

Gloom surrounded them. There was the wailing of children who had died in infancy and had never had a chance to enjoy life. There were those who, although innocent of wrongdoing, had been falsely accused and had been put to death. There were those who had died by their own hands, and those who had been slain in war—dead Greeks as well as Trojans milled around Aeneas. There were the cries of criminals, eternally tortured, kept here by the Furies, who used writhing serpents for whips. Lastly, and most pathetically, there were those who had killed themselves for love. Among them Aeneas saw Dido, and he was filled with pity and remorse.

"Dido!" he cried, approaching her. "Can it be true that I was the cause of your death? I never would believe it. The gods know I left you unwillingly. I swear I loved you more than can be told, but I was forced to obey the dictates of the oracle. Tell me you understand. Say you forgive me."

Dido did not answer. Without a word, without even looking at him, she turned away. Aeneas would have pursued her, but the Sibyl shook her head.

"There is little time left," she said. "You have seen enough sadness and cruelty, horror and misery. We shall leave these scenes for a happier domain, for Elysium, the abode of the blest." In Elysium were the spirits of those who had done good and even great things on earth—upright and noble beings, champions of large causes, priests and poets—all those who had deserved a lasting bliss. Among them, Aeneas saw his father, Anchises, and rushed to embrace him.

"O my son," cried Anchises, "how I have worried for you! And how I rejoiced when you passed through your perils! I need worry no longer. There is still much to be done, much to be overcome, but there is nothing that will stand in the way of your triumph. You will found a nation. It will be called Rome, and you will rule it by your authority. Your descendants will be Romans, and they will

wage war against the wicked, spare the conquered, and bring peace
to the world."

Happy in the thought of so glorious a future, Aeneas returned to
earth. Taking leave of the Sibyl, he and his Trojans settled near the
mouth of the Tiber river. Their achievements so impressed the king
of Latium that he offered Aeneas his daughter, Lavinia, in marriage.
This infuriated several of the nearby chiefs, especially Turnus, who
considered himself engaged to Lavinia. He summoned the clan
leaders for a council of war.

"The strangers must be driven from our land," Turnus told them.
"The Trojans are an aggressive lot, but we too can be militant.
Joined as allies, we can overcome them."

Fighting broke out at once. The Trojans were outnumbered, but
they were not outfought. The conflict grew in fury. There were
minor skirmishes and major battles. Boats filled with armed warriors
ranged the Tiber for the first time. Bands of cavalry struck at each
other, the horses' hooves trampling the ground with fierce four-
footed strokes. Men slaughtered each other and torrents of blood
stained the earth. When it became evident that neither side was
winning, Aeneas challenged Turnus to single combat. Turnus was
forced to accept.

The struggle was short. Turnus was soon wounded and Aeneas
would have spared him, but he saw that Turnus was wearing the
armor of a slain Trojan. Enraged, he thrust his sword through the
enemy's heart.

This ended the war. Aeneas married Lavinia, built his promised
city, and named it Lavinium. The oracle's prophecy had been fulfilled. Aeneas had found the birthplace of his ancestors, the place
that was to become Rome.

SYBARIS

... *Life of Luxury*

F ALL the ancient cities Sybaris was the least indus-
trious and the most prosperous. Its richest provinces
were poor compared to Sybaris itself. So fond were
its citizens of carefree living that even today people
who dislike work and delight only in pleasure are
called sybarites. It was said that other people ate to
live but that the people of Sybaris lived to eat. They drank from
golden goblets and dined off silver plates. They ate five times a day,
and every one of their meals was a banquet. Cooks were considered
more important than councillors of state, and the one who invented
a new sauce was the celebrity of the week.

The Sybarites were as fond of fine clothes as they were of food.
The men paraded the streets in expensive foreign fabrics while the
women lolled in filmy gauze at home. Purple, royal purple, was their
favorite color, although cloth of gold was worn for celebrations.

Next to eating and dressing-up—primping and preening were
favorite pastimes—they loved sleeping. An owner of an estate that
employed a thousand slaves boasted that he had never seen the
sun rise and that the way to live long was to sleep long, ten or
twelve hours a day.

The Sybarites hated noise and refused to keep anything that might
bark, whistle, cry, or call. Hens were allowed, but no roosters. Crows
who liked to roost were detested as much as roosters who liked to
crow. Sybarites pampered themselves with every conceivable comfort. According to Seneca (one of the more austere philosophers), a
Sybarite woke up screaming in the middle of the night because, she
claimed, a heavy weight had fallen on her. It turned out to be a rose
petal.

Like all other Greek cities, Sybaris had an army. But it seemed less important to have the soldiers properly armed than to have them beautifully costumed. And so with the cavalry. The horses wore plumed headgear and were trained to dance to music.

That was their undoing. When a rival city attacked Sybaris, the soldiers were so afraid of soiling their clothes that they declined to fight, and when dance music was played by the attackers—some traitor had informed the enemy—the horses refused to obey their riders and danced right into the enemy's ranks. As a consequence, the Sybarites suffered a terrible defeat. Their city was destroyed; nothing was left but tumbled walls.

All this happened more than two thousand years ago. Centuries passed; winds and rains brought soil to cover the ruins; the very outlines of the town disappeared. To some it seemed that Sybaris had existed only in the imagination of a poet or in the mind of some historian who loved mystery better than history.

Then, a few years ago, a band of stubborn archeologists located the city. It was twenty feet below the surface of the earth in southern Italy which the Greeks had colonized eight centuries before the Christian era. Soundings were made; plans were drawn; diggers were put to work. Sooner or later they hope to find a golden goblet, a silver plate, or some other evidence that the people of Sybaris were as luxury-loving as sybarites are supposed to be.

SOCRATES

... *The Cup of Hemlock*

E WAS an ugly little man—the nostrils of his snub nose flared, his small eyes squinted, his stomach bulged. Nevertheless, he was not only admired but adored. He had the look of a satyr and the soul of a saint. A teacher who lived almost two thousand five hundred years ago, Socrates taught that all men respond to goodness and that they long for two things: truth and beauty. He insisted that truth *is* beauty, a conclusion that Keats echoed in the last lines of his "Ode on a Grecian Urn":

"Beauty is truth, truth beauty"—that is all
Ye know on earth, and all ye need to know.

Socrates was not only a great teacher but also a great talker. He never wrote anything down, but his inspired talks were recorded by Plato, the philosopher, and Xenophon, the historian. His disciples worshiped him; soldiers and statesmen, eager youths and wise old men gathered to listen to his discourses. His mother had been a midwife, and he said, like her, he was helping others to give birth to new ideas. He welcomed differences of opinion. He went about asking questions, prompting people to look into their methods, their motives, and themselves. He urged the young not to accept easy solutions, but to explore unknown fields, to continue to learn by questioning everything. "Knowledge is virtue," he said. "Ignorance is vice."

It was Socrates' quest for knowledge, with his devotion to unflinching honesty, that was his undoing. He was charged with heresy, with failure to worship the gods, and with corrupting the morals of

youth. Socrates defended himself by saying that his whole life had been devoted to a search for the basic truth in all things, and that he could not give up this search even if it cost him his life.

"If you will release me on condition that I abandon my pursuit of what is good for mankind, I would reply that I cannot accept the offer. As long as I live I must oppose what is base, and I must expose whatever is false. Nothing you can do can make me alter my determination to try to make men strive for wisdom and worship truth. You cannot escape guilt, and you are guilty when you turn away from the life of truth."

His accusers were outraged at what they considered Socrates' obstinacy. "He is not only stubborn," they said; "he is also insolent. He has turned his back on us as well as on the gods. He must die."

Socrates accepted the verdict calmly. He was put in prison, his leg was chained, and, though friends arranged to bribe the jailor, he refused to escape. "I am faced with death," he told them, "and I must submit to my punishment. My accusers have succumbed to wickedness; they must face theirs."

His favorite disciple, Plato, described the last day of his life in a work called *Phaido*. Unperturbed, Socrates talked with those who had come to be with him during his last hours just as he had talked with them on the street or in his home. He spoke about the good life and about death as a natural consequence of life. He spoke about the burial of the body and the immortality of the spirit. His disciples wept, but Socrates reproved them. "Do not agitate yourselves," he told them. "Death is not a time for agony; it is a time for peace."

Toward evening the jailor came with a cup of hemlock. He, too, wept. "Do not hold this against me," he said. "I did not brew this poison. Others planned it, not I."

Socrates smiled, rubbed his leg where the chains had chafed it, and drank every drop in the fatal cup. "The hour of departure has arrived," he said. "We go our separate ways—I to die and you to live. Which is the better, God only knows." Those were his last words.

APOLLO AND DAPHNE

...The Laurel Wreath

HEN the Romans conquered Greece they took over the Greek gods. They kept the gods' characters and characteristics, but they changed the names. Zeus became Jupiter, Hera became Juno, Poseidon became Neptune, Ares became Mars, Artemis became Diana, Aphrodite became Venus, Athene became Minerva, Hermes became Mercury, Dionysus became Bacchus, Eros became Cupid. Apollo remained Apollo.

Ivory-limbed, golden-haired, Apollo was the fairest and the most beloved of the Olympians. He was irresistible to all—to all except an earth-born nymph, Daphne, daughter of a river god. For this the mischievous Cupid was to blame.

Cupid was sharpening his arrows and fitting a new string to his bow when Apollo approached.

"You are too young to play with dangerous toys," said Apollo. "Warlike instruments are for those who know how to handle them and who know what power they have."

"Young I may be," replied Cupid, "but my weapons are not toys. The arrows I shoot do not draw blood, but they have more power than yours. Let me show you."

He took a little golden dart from his quiver and aimed it at Apollo. It struck, and Apollo laughed, for he felt no pain. At that moment he glanced down, saw Daphne, and sensed an intense burning in his heart. He had fallen suddenly and violently in love.

To make it harder for Apollo, Cupid took another arrow—a leaden one—and let it fly at Daphne. This arrow inspired fear instead of love, and the instant the nymph saw Apollo she turned and ran.

66

"Stay!" cried Apollo. "I would not harm you. You are the loveliest thing that earth ever bore. The slenderest tree has not your grace; the brightest stars lack the glow of your eyes; no rose or violet can match your fragrance. Let me hold you. You shun me like a frightened faun, but I am no beast to scare you, no lion that would tear you. On the contrary I am a god, a god who would give you love forever."

Daphne did not reply but ran still faster. Her garments streamed as the wind blew her unbound hair about her. She looked more desirable than ever. Apollo cried out again.

"Hear me! I am the god of the sun, but the heavens will be dark if you turn away. I am the god of song, yet I will not sing again if you do not answer. I am the god of medicine, but I know no way to cure myself; only you can heal my hurt."

By this time Daphne's strength had begun to fail and Apollo was near enough to touch her. As soon as she felt his hands upon her, Daphne cried out to the river. "Help me, Father! Open the earth, let your waters take me! Cover me! Spirit me away, or change my form which has caused this trouble!"

Apollo caught her in his arms, but he held something strange. Her breast was covered with a woody growth, her fingers turned into twigs, green leaves sprouted from her head, and her feet that had run so swiftly stood rooted in earth. Apollo realized he was embracing a tree, a slender sensitive laurel which trembled as though it were still flesh.

"Alas," sighed Apollo. "I would have made you my wife. But if I cannot have you as my bride, you shall be my tree. No tree will ever be like it. Your leaves will stay green through the fiercest winter, and I will wear them as a crown. They will be woven into wreaths, and they will be placed as trophies on the brows of those who deserve honor. Only those who truly triumph will be worthy of a wreath of laurel."

Apollo stopped speaking and the tree, bowing its head, lowered its leaves about him.

ORPHEUS

... The Fabulous Musician

E WAS unlike other heroes. Son of Apollo, Orpheus was no warrior, no adventurer, no slayer of mythical beasts. Inheriting a love of music from his father, he played the lute so marvelously that howling wolves would keep still and gather around to listen to him. Lions, purring, would rub against his shoulders. It was said that when he sang, trees would follow wherever he went, rivers would change their courses, rocks would echo every note, the rough billows of the sea would pause, cease pounding, and lie quiet on the sands.

Music made Orpheus as joyful as the things he charmed. Nothing interrupted his happiness until the day that his beloved wife Eurydice was bitten by a snake and died. His bright world went dark. He stopped singing; he could not eat or drink; he could not sleep. He could not live without Eurydice. There was only one thing for him to do. He determined to go down to the domain of the dead and reclaim his wife.

When he came to the gate of the Underworld, the three-headed watchdog Cerberus threatened him. But Orpheus remembered his music. He sang, and Cerberus wagged its tail and extended a paw. Still singing, Orpheus passed among those condemned to labor without relief through eternity. In Hell his music brought moments of hope. Thirsting Tantalus (whose plight gave us the word "tantalize"), standing in water that receded whenever he bent down to drink, listened and forgot about his eternal thirst even though the water stood still so as not to disturb Orpheus' singing. The stone that panting Sisyphus continually had to push uphill, only to have

it roll down again, remained motionless and, for a moment, Sisyphus
relaxed. The avenging Furies stopped thinking about punishments
and, for the first time, smiled. Unopposed, Orpheus faced Pluto,
king of the Underworld.

"It is a miracle that you, a living man, should be here," said King
Pluto. "What brings you to the world of the dead?"

"One thing only," said Orpheus. "The one thing I cannot live
without. I have come for Eurydice, my wife, who came to you too
soon. Love guided me all the way. Give her to me. Let her live out
a mortal's term of life, and when she returns to you I will go with
her."

Pluto was touched. He, too, knew what love was, for love had made him carry off the flower-fair Proserpine who had become his queen. Iron tears wet his cheeks.

"For love's sake I grant your wish. But it is granted on one condition. You had no right to be here, no right to see what you have seen. So you are not to look back until you have reached the upper world. Should you look back you will lose Eurydice."

Pluto gave a sign and Eurydice, still limping from the snake bite, stood beside her husband. Orpheus led the way through the underground passages and Eurydice followed. He remembered Pluto's warning and he kept his eyes sternly ahead. However, when he reached the gate he grew impatient and, wanting to assure himself that Eurydice was still there, he turned around to tell her that they had come through. There she was. But before he could speak, she sighed, faded, and was drawn back to the abode of the dead. A whisper hung in the air: "Farewell. Farewell. A last farewell."

Somehow Orpheus managed to stumble back to earth. Once there, he was alone more than ever. He wandered about unconsolably. He avoided the company of men and women. Only his music gave him occasional comfort.

One day as he was playing sadly on his lute, a group of wild Bacchantes tried to draw him into their revels. He refused to join them and they grew angry.

"He thinks he's too good for us!" cried one, and aimed a stone at his head. Others began to throw things—rocks, clubs, spears— but the missiles refused to touch the fabulous singer. Anything thrown fell at his feet.

Then the Bacchantes started to scream, and their outcries deadened the sound of the music. Orpheus was helpless. The stones they now threw struck him. He fell and, like maniacs, the Bacchantes tore the singer to pieces. Not content with killing him, they threw him in the river and flung his lute after him. It was said that the lute continued to play and Orpheus' lips never stopped making music.

Once more Orpheus entered the Underworld. This time he came to find his place in the kingdom of Hades. Eurydice was there to meet him. Separated in life, they were reunited by death.

MIDAS

... The Greed for Gold

"NOTHING," according to an old saying, "can ever satisfy a greedy man." The proverb is proved by the story of King Midas.

Some Phrygian peasants found a man sleeping in their vineyards. The man felt he had every right to be there—after all, he was the god of wine, and he had been drinking. His hair was matted, his clothes were dirty, and he looked like some vagabond. Suspicious, the peasants bound his wrists and brought him to Midas, king of Phrygia. Midas recognized him at once.

"Untie his hands," he commanded. "This is no common person. This is Bacchus, the god who blesses your vines, who sees that the sun ripens your grapes and gives you a good harvest."

The king not only rescued him but entertained him lavishly for weeks. At the end of the time Bacchus said, "It is within my power to fulfill any desire you may have. What would you wish for most?"

Midas was a very rich man, but being greedy, he felt he was not nearly rich enough. He did not hesitate, but said at once, "I wish that everything I touch would turn to gold."

"It is a strange wish," said Bacchus. "But it is granted. No matter what you touch, it will immediately become gold."

Midas was delighted. He began experimenting. He broke off an olive branch, and the stem and gray leaves became a golden spray. He picked up a pebble and it changed into a little ball of gold. He put a finger to a rose and its petals were heavy with gold. He went from tree to tree, touching and turning them into a stiff solid gold forest. He put his palm against his palace walls and his palace burned with a golden glow.

Joyfully he ordered a sumptuous repast and sat down to enjoy it. The goblet immediately became gold. But as soon as his lips touched the wine, he choked; what went into his mouth was not a liquid but hard metal, precious no doubt but scarcely something to drink. And so with the food. The bread he took up became a piece of gold. The peas were gold pellets in his mouth. The meat would have broken his teeth had he tried to chew it. He staggered from the table.

"I shall starve!" he cried. "The gift was not a blessing but a curse! I shall be killed with gold!"

Frantically he sought Bacchus. "Help me!" he cried. "If you do not, I shall die."

"What troubles you so?" asked Bacchus.

"Your gift," said Midas bitterly. "No one can eat or drink gold!"

Bacchus smiled. "I thought you would tire of the golden touch. It is often sad not to get everything you wish, but it is sometimes sadder to get it. If you want to get rid of the power, go to the river Pactolus. Wash your body in the deepest part of the stream. The sands will change into gold, but you will be cleansed and free of the fatal charm."

Once cured, Midas hated the sight of gold. He turned away from all shows of wealth and went to live in the woods where he became a follower of Pan, god of the flocks, fields, and forests.

It was his loyalty to Pan that got him into trouble again. Pan had invented a musical instrument he called a syrinx. It was made out of hollow reeds and it became known as Pan's pipes. He played so well and was so much praised that he dared to challenge Apollo to a contest. Besides being the sun god, Apollo was the god of music and his playing charmed not only the Olympian gods but all living things. An umpire was chosen and Pan began.

As Pan blew on his pipes the wildest creatures came out of the field and forest. Moles crept from their holes; rabbits gathered in a circle about him; even bears left their caves and sat on their haunches to hear. Leaves rustled happily. It was as if all nature were applauding.

Then Apollo took up his lyre and swept the strings. With the first chord a trembling ran through the earth. Never had the world known such music. Everything—beast, bird, and blossom—turned to Apollo. The air vibrated with joy. There could be no question about the verdict.

But Midas objected. "I say nothing against Apollo," he muttered, "but I prefer Pan."

Apollo smiled grimly. "I'm afraid you haven't much of an ear for music, my friend. I'll give you a better one—in fact I'll give you a pair of ears, bigger as well as better ones."

Midas felt his ears grow longer and looser. They began to waggle. He realized he now had the ears of a jackass.

What to do? How could he hide his disgrace? He wrapped his head in a huge turban and never took it off in public. But, though he could conceal his shame from the court, he could not hide it from the barber who dressed his hair.

"If you mention this—er—accident to anyone," Midas told him, "you will lose not only your position but your head."

For a long time the barber kept the secret to himself. Finally the temptation to talk about it was too much for him. He went to the riverside, dug a hole in the earth, and breathed into it. "Hush! Hush!" he whispered. "It's a secret! Midas has ears like a jackass!" Then he filled up the hole and felt relieved.

But the earth remembered. Reeds grew from the hole and, with the least stir of wind, they rustled and murmured. Gossiping to each other, the reeds repeated what they had heard. Again and again they whispered, "Hush! Hush! It's a secret! Midas has ears like a jackass!" They never stopped talking about it.

CUPID AND PSYCHE

...The Trial of Love

SYCHE was so incredibly beautiful that the goddess of beauty grew jealous. She complained to her son, the winged Cupid.

"Men are not only admiring her but worshiping her," said Venus. "They even call her their 'soul.' This cannot be permitted. She must be punished."

"But how?" asked Cupid.

"By piercing her heart with one of your arrows so that she will fall helplessly in love. Then, as the arrow begins to do its work, see to it that she falls in love with someone unsightly or even beastly. Look!" said Venus, pointing to where Psyche sat in her garden. "That is the upstart girl who has been compared to me!"

Cupid looked and, for the first time in his life, the god of love fell helplessly in love. He knew he could do only part of what his mother commanded. He would make the girl fall in love, but he could not hurt or humiliate her.

Meanwhile, Psyche was deriving no pleasure from her beauty. Men thought her too lovely to live with, and she remained unmarried. Her father appealed to the gods. The answer that came was puzzling.

"Let the maiden be arrayed for marriage and for death. Let her be placed on a mountaintop and abide there for what fate may follow."

It was an unhappy procession that ascended the mountain. At first the marriage torches burned brightly, but soon the smoke turned black as a funeral pall. The fresh flowers on the bridal veil withered. When they reached the peak, Psyche kissed her two older

sisters and her parents, whispered a final farewell, and lay down on
the grass as though on a bier.

It was then that a soft breeze touched the girl and, without dis-
turbing her thin white garments, breathed delicately upon her
until she fell asleep.

When Psyche woke she imagined she was in the abode of one
of the gods. Before her eyes there stood a palace so noble that it
could not have been built by human hands. Psyche marveled and,
as she rose to her feet, the door opened and she heard a voice like
music.

"Welcome to your home, fair bride," it said. "We have been waiting for you. Soon a royal supper will be served. You are tired now,
so lie down awhile. When you rise a perfumed bath will be ready
for you."

Bewildered, Psyche felt that her senses were playing tricks on her
mind. The excitement was wearying and, believing she was in the
midst of a dream, she sank on a silken bed. Gradually she realized
everything she thought she had dreamed was true. The bath was
real and comforting; the dinner, consisting of her favorite dishes,
was magnificent; the musicians, a great number of them, sang en-
chantingly. There was only one flaw. She could see no one. Loving
but unseen hands washed her; the dishes were wafted through the
air; the music-makers were invisible.

When Psyche retired to her bedroom it was dark. In the darkness
the bridegroom came, and in the darkness she became his bride. She
heard his voice—the voice of love—but she could not see his features.
And with the first streak of dawn he disappeared.

So it was for days and nights. Luxury, beauty, music, and love.
Then one night her husband, holding her close, said, "My darling,
I must warn you. Your sisters have grown suspicious. They will visit
the mountaintop to see what has become of you. If you should hear
lamentations or any other sound of sorrow, do not answer. If you do,
it may cause trouble and even bring destruction upon us." Psyche
promised to do as he advised, and once more he vanished before
daylight without showing his face.

As predicted, the sisters climbed the mountain and, seeing no
trace of Psyche, broke into outcries. Psyche, unable to console them,
spent the day weeping in her room. Deprived of human conversation
she felt she was a prisoner, even though her prison was a palace.

That night her unseen husband felt her tremble. "Dearest Psyche,"
he said, "what will become of our joy if, even in my arms, you feel

grief? I cannot bear to see you in pain. If it is because you cannot meet your sisters, I release you from your promise. Do as you wish. But I must warn you that you may do something dangerous, even disastrous. You may have your sisters here; you may give them anything you fancy. But—it may sound harsh—do not trust them. Above all, do not answer any questions about me or about my bodily form. If you yield to their curiosity—or your own—we may never embrace each other again."

"Oh my dearest, my breath of life, my other soul," exclaimed Psyche. "I would die a thousand deaths rather than lose your love. I would not exchange your embraces for those of a god, not even those of Cupid himself! You are my heart of hearts, and I know you have granted my desire to see my sisters because of our great love and your great goodness. I will remember. I will bear in mind what you told me."

Again they kissed, again he held her through the night, and again, toward morning, he melted unseen from her arms.

The next day Psyche opened the door and, proud as any mistress of a new home, showed her sisters the beauties of her golden house. She displayed her ravishing dresses, treated them to a concert by invisible musicians, and entertained them at a delicious dinner.

"How fortunate you are," exclaimed the sisters. "How lucky to have such a rich and wonderful husband. Tell us something about him. What does he look like? What does he do?"

"Oh," said Psyche, recalling her loved one's warning but unable to keep silent, "he is young, very young, and very handsome. He is a hunter—that is why he is away so much of the time." Then, feeling she might betray herself and let slip the secret of her husband's appearing only when it was dark, she turned the conversation to other matters, gave them gifts of jewelry, and let them go.

As soon as they were alone the sisters complained to each other. "What a shame!" said the first. "We, her older sisters, are married off to men who expect us to wait on them, while she is served by a hundred willing hands!"

"A young husband, too!" rejoined the other sister. "My husband is old enough to be my father and he is balder than a squash. I spend most of my time massaging him, soiling my hands with greasy rags and smelly lotions."

"Did you notice," said the first, "how she walked over the jeweled pavement as though she had always walked on floors of gold?"

"And did *you* notice how she flung a few things at us and hurried us off? I would not be a woman if I did not resent it."

"Yes," nodded the first. "Let us go back to our households and think of some way to punish her for her grand airs!"

That night Psyche's husband warned her again: "Peril is coming closer. Those sisters of yours who pretend to love you are scheming against you. At this very moment they are plotting your ruin. They will come again, and they will try to trap you into talk. Do not be drawn into conversation on any subject with them. If you *must* talk, do not enter into any discussion about me. You are little more than a child, but soon you will have a child of your own. If your sisters succeed, I will have to leave both of you."

Blissfully excited that she was to be a mother, Psyche assured him that she would never do anything contrary to his wishes. Then she began figuring how long it would be before the time would come when she would be happier than even a goddess could be. Her joyful mood was marred when her sisters paid a second visit. They pretended to be delighted with the news. "Our little sister," they cooed falsely, "is growing up fast. What a blessing she sheds on everything, and what a blessing she will bring into the world."

So, dissembling their intention, little by little, they beguiled her into talk of the future.

"And the child's father," said the oldest sister. "How proud he will be. I wonder whether it will resemble him."

"Yes," added the other, "a man always looks for resemblances. What," she went on guilefully, "does your husband really look like?"

Taken off guard and forgetting what she had answered last time, Psyche replied, "He is nearly middle-aged; there are a few gray hairs scattered on his head."

"And what does he do?" insisted the oldest sister.

"He is a merchant," said Psyche. "A very wealthy merchant who carries on a great trade and has to travel much of the time." Then, afraid of having gone too far, she again gave them gifts and kissed them good-by.

The sisters could not wait to vent their jealousy. "What a story!" cried one. "First she said her husband was a young man; now she says he is middle-aged. First he was a hunter; now he is a merchant. Either she is lying to protect herself from something, or she has never seen him, or there is no husband at all. In any case, she is a wicked creature who does not deserve what she has."

"But," said the other, "it may be that she is married to a god and cannot tell us about it."

"All the more reason," said the first, "why she should be humbled. If she is really married to a god and bears a godly child, it would make us look smaller than ever. I could not bear it. Nor could you. We must act—humiliate her, destroy her if necessary. Whatever we do, we must do it at once."

That night Psyche was full of gay prattle. But Cupid scarcely listened. After she had told him for the tenth time how joyful she felt and how delighted her sisters were, he spoke. "The hour has come," he said slowly, "the hour of decision. Your evil sisters are preparing your doom. They will come once more and try to poison your mind. They will tell you things too terrible to believe, but they will expect you to believe them. It is you who must withstand them. Be on your guard, my best beloved. Otherwise—" He left the sentence unfinished.

Next morning the sisters arrived. Without waiting to be greeted they began. "O dear sister, how we suffer for you! We who watch over you are distressed by the danger you are in. We have guessed to our sorrow"—here they shed a few hypocritical tears—"that your husband never shows himself because he is too terrible to be seen. You tell us he is both young and old. If that is so, it is perhaps because he can change his form at will. You say he is away hunting or trading most of the time. But what if he hunts victims! And what if he trades in human flesh! It breaks our hearts to say it, but your husband may be a monster. At any time he may devour you. He may wait until you become a mother before he feasts upon both you and your child, or he may strike tonight. Do as you will—or do nothing—but do not say that we failed to warn you in time."

Hearing this distracted Psyche. She did not know what to say or what to think. "It is true," she said to herself, "that I have never seen my husband. I do not even know what kind of a man he is— if he *is* a man."

Turning to her sisters, she said, "You frighten me. But what can I do?"

"We have thought of a way to save you," they said craftily. "Take a sharp knife to bed with you; hide it well. Take also a lamp full of oil, and, after trimming it so that its light is low, conceal it behind the bed-curtain. When his breathing tells you he is asleep, slip out of bed, pick up the lamp, and plunge in the knife. Then you can return to your father's house, and we will help you find a human being for a husband."

Night came, and with it came the bridegroom. He was not his usual rapturous self; after the first embrace he fell asleep. Weak in body but strong in purpose, driven by her need to know the worst, Psyche left the bed and found what she needed in the darkness. She held the knife in one hand and the lamp in the other. The light was feeble, but what she saw made her gasp. She almost fainted; she could not believe her senses. In the dim glow she beheld the most wonderful vision—the young god of love, the Golden Boy himself!

At the sight, her heart bounded and the very flame of the lamp leaped up eagerly. There, just as Cupid had always been pictured, were the sun-curled locks, the flushed cheeks, the alabaster neck, and, on his shoulders, shining wings of the purest white. The wings were folded, but along the outer edge the small feathers trembled as though awaiting flight. Psyche felt so ashamed, so guilty, that she would have plunged the knife in her own breast. But the knife, unwilling to perform such a crime, twisted itself out of her hand and fell clattering to the floor. The lamp shook in her hand and a drop of burning oil fell on the shoulder of the sleeping god. He sprang from the bed, his wings stirred into motion and, poised in air, he spoke sadly.

"Foolish girl, you have punished me as well as yourself. I disobeyed my mother who commanded me to make you fall in love with someone low and loathsome. Instead, I fell in love with you myself. I tried to put you on your guard, but I failed. All of us will be punished. For the evil your sisters tried to make you commit they will be punished in a terrible way. You will be punished only by being left alone."

There was a flurry of wings and a feather brushed her cheek. Then she was truly alone. She ran from the room. She had only one idea; she would have to find Cupid and ask his forgiveness.

He was not to be found, for he lay in his mother's house sick at heart. Instead of trying to comfort him, Venus scolded.

"You should be ashamed of yourself," she said. "If you *had* to fall in love, you might at least have fallen in love with a minor goddess or one of my own Graces, instead of a common girl. And, of all girls, the very one who is said to rival your mother! Far from making her fall in love with some lout as I ordered, you marry her yourself, and present me with a daughter-in-law I loathe! I will make you and your precious darling suffer for this. I will go to Juno herself. The empress of the gods will see to it that your pretty looks—

the golden hairs which I have curled so often with my own hands—are cut off. She will clip your wings and break your bow!"

But Juno would not side with Venus. "Cupid is no longer a child," she said mildly. "Besides, is falling in love a crime? If it is," she said slyly, "even goddesses have been known to commit it. Surely you should be the first to understand Cupid's weakness. Or should we call it a romantic disposition he had inherited? After all, he is his mother's son."

Meanwhile, Psyche was wandering from place to place. "If," she said to herself, "Cupid will not take me back as his wife, he may accept me as his slave. I would serve him all the rest of my life."

Finally it occurred to her that he might be in his mother's home. Summoning all her courage she struggled until she reached the abode of Venus. There she faced the goddess.

"So," said Venus angrily. "You have decided to pay your respects to your mother-in-law. Or did you expect to be welcomed by your sick husband who lies ill because of your baseness? Well, we shall see what kind of a daughter-in-law you may be after I am through with you!"

"I will do anything you say," said Psyche tearfully. "Anything."

"Very well," said Venus. "We shall see how obedient and how clever you are. I shall test your ability as a housewife. To begin with, here are a mixed lot of seeds—wheat, barley, millet, vetch, and poppy. Sort them out for me. Separate them grain by grain—and have it done by dusk."

Stunned by the impossibility of the task, Psyche sat hopelessly in front of the disordered heap. Then a little ant, seeing what had happened, took pity on her. Calling his fellow workers, he instructed them. "This forlorn girl is the wife of the god of Love, and she is in great danger. Like us, she is a creature of earth, and she needs our help." Immediately the six-footed insects sped to the heap and, in an hour, all the different grains were arranged in separate piles.

When Venus saw what had been accomplished she was angrier than ever. "You never did this by yourself. Someone you have somehow pleased did it for you. But I am not through with you. Do you see that grove along the riverbank? Among the trees are a flock of savage sheep with golden wool. Tomorrow you must fetch me some of that precious fleece."

Knowing she could never satisfy Venus, Psyche was in despair. She went to the riverside and thought of drowning herself. But a little wind among the reeds spoke and told her what to do.

"Stay here until the sun begins to go down. In the heat of the day those sheep are violent; their horns are razor sharp and their bite is poisonous. In late afternoon they sleep in the shade. At that time you will find, sticking to shrubs and branches, more of the fleece than you need."

When Psyche brought back handfuls of the golden stuff, Venus once more shook her head. "Again you have been helped," she said scornfully. "This time you will be tested for solitary courage. Do you see that dark mountain? At the summit there is a cave. In the cave is a black stream that flows down to the regions of the dead. Take this small pitcher and bring it back full of that icy water."

Psyche climbed among slippery rocks until she reached the top. There were dragon-like snakes and other threatening creatures confronting her. "Depart or die!" they screamed at her. "If you touch one drop of the deadly water you are doomed!"

It was then that Jupiter's bird, the lordly eagle, came to her rescue. "Poor innocent," he said. "Did you hope to take water from the Styx? Even the mighty Jupiter would not touch one drop of that relentless stream. But I cannot be harmed. Let me have your pitcher." He took the vessel, filled it to the brim, and, flying over the heads of the dragons, brought it safely back.

Venus was infuriated. "You are very clever," she said guilefully. "You probably are a witch. Well, there is one more thing to be undertaken. I will not be appeased until you deliver this box to Proserpine. She is the queen of Hades, the land of the dead. You must tell her that Venus requests some of her beauty, for I have wasted much of my own beauty taking care of a sick son. She will put some beautifier in the box. Then hurry back."

Psyche knew that this was the end. Bidding her descend to the pit of Hades, Venus had given Psyche a death warrant. She climbed to the top of a tower intending to hurl herself from it, and thus descend straightway to the regions of the dead. But the tower spoke and said:

"Foolish one, do not give up hope. If you destroy yourself, you will surely go to the Underworld and you will never return. Listen to me. Remember the mountain with the cave containing a hole that leads to Hades? Follow along that opening. It is a rough passage, for it takes you down to the secret river of the dead. Do not go emptyhanded. Take a barley-cake soaked in honey and two pieces of money. When you come to the Styx, the river of the dead, give one of your coins to Charon, the ghostly ferryman. He will take you across. Then you will face Cerberus, the watchdog of Hades. Throw him the cake and he will let you pass into the presence of Proserpine. Deliver your message, and take whatever Proserpine will give you. But do not open the box that contains the beauty secret."

Psyche took heart. She followed the tower's instructions and all went well. Proserpine was kind. She did what Psyche requested and wished her good fortune. After Psyche had given her other coin to Cerberus and was past the limits of the Underworld, she considered the box. "There is nothing wrong in borrowing just a little of the beauty of the gods," she thought. "I would like to seem more beautiful when I meet my beloved." But when the box was opened all it contained was a drowsy vapor. The beautifier was sleep—and Psyche sank to the ground in a deep slumber.

In the meantime Cupid, recovering from his hurt, his wings strengthened, flew through the window of the room where his mother had kept him. He sought out Psyche and his instinct brought him quickly to the spot where she lay motionless. Shaking the sleep from her, he comforted his beloved, told her she need have no further fear of Venus, and carried her up to the high heavens.

There he appealed to Jupiter. "You have not always paid me proper respect." Jupiter frowned. "In fact, you have often wounded me with those arrows of yours; they have made me fall in love too frequently." Then he smiled. "Nevertheless, because I am by nature soft-hearted, I will help you."

Ordering all the gods to attend, he addressed the august assembly. "Mighty ones," he said, "you are well acquainted with this naughty youth. He has disobeyed his mother; he is wild and willful; his actions are lawless. He should certainly be restrained—and I cannot think of a better way of accomplishing this than by marriage. He shall marry his Psyche and be subject to the woman he has chosen. As for you," he continued, speaking to Venus, "you need not worry that you will be disgraced because your son has married a mortal. I will confer immortality upon her." Then he turned to Psyche. "Drink this, my dear," he said, offering her a cup of ambrosia, "and you will be one of us. Cupid will never leave you again, and you will enjoy an eternal honeymoon in heaven."

PERSEUS

... *The Head of Medusa*

 EDUSA was once the loveliest of girls. She was also the vainest. In love with her own charms, especially her hair which fell in a shower of gold to her waist, she boasted that no goddess could surpass her beauty. This offended Minerva who decreed that no man would ever again look at Medusa with pleasure. The goddess changed the girl into a hideous monster and transformed her glorious golden hair into yellow snakes. To make the punishment more severe, the sight of Medusa was literally petrifying. Any man who looked at her was turned to stone.

Perseus was the son of Danae and Jupiter. He was called the Sun Prince, for the god had come to Danae in a rain of sunbeams. Mother and child had been adopted by a powerful but hard-hearted king, and when Perseus was fully grown he wanted to show he was grateful.

"Name something—anything—you desire and I will get it for you," said Perseus in a burst of youthful confidence. "I will get it no matter what or where it is."

"Very well," said the king, who was secretly jealous of the youth and wanted him out of the way. "Bring me the head of Medusa."

Perseus could not believe what he had heard. He knew that no man had ever dared meet Medusa's eyes, much less confront her with a weapon. Heartsick, he wandered to the shore and sat disconsolately on the sands. He did not notice a fisherman standing near until he was asked why he seemed troubled. When Perseus told what the king had requested, the fisherman shook his head.

"It is a terrible thing to demand, and yours is an almost impossible

86

quest. I said 'almost,' for I have something which may be of help. It is nothing but a leather pouch, but you will find it useful one day."

Perseus stared as the fisherman put out a hand and plucked a bag-like object from the air. The youth's eyes almost left their sockets when the fisherman's coarse cloak fell off revealing a silver breastplate, while his cap became a golden helmet, and an unearthly light surrounded his body. Perseus knew it must be Mercury.

"Yes," said the transformed fisherman. "I am the messenger of the gods, especially of one god. That god is your father. Jupiter has watched you grow into manhood. He is pleased, and he will let nothing harmful happen to you. However, what is to be done must be done by you yourself. To perform your task you need three things: a brass shield bright as a mirror, a pair of sandals which will let you fly through the air, and a sword-like sickle which can cut through anything with a single stroke."

"But where," asked Perseus, "can I find those things?"

"At the western rim of the world sit the Gray Women," said Mercury. "There are three of them. They were born old and gray and wrinkled, and they have only one eye among them. They know where the things you need are hidden. They will not tell you unless you persuade or compel them. You are not allowed to hurt them. You must be clever. Go, and see what you can do."

It was many days and many nights before Perseus reached the twilight land which is at the western rim of the world. There, as Mercury had foretold, sat the three Gray Women mumbling to each other.

"Someone is coming," said the first. "I can feel his approach."

"Someone is coming," said the second. "I can hear his footsteps."

"Someone is coming," said the third. "I can see him with my eye."

"Let us see him, too," said the first and second. "Pass us the eye."

As soon as the third Gray Woman held it toward the others, Perseus snatched it. The three gave a woeful cry.

"It has happened! The thing we have always dreaded has happened! The eye has been stolen! Now none of us can see! Give it back! Give it back!"

"You can have it back if you will do one thing for me," said Perseus. "Tell me where three things I need are hidden: a brass shield bright as a mirror, a pair of sandals so I can fly through the air, and a sword-like sickle that can cut through anything."

"It is a secret we swore never to disclose," said the first Gray Women. "But we are sightless and helpless without our eye. Listen, then. You must travel southward thirty days until you come to an island with a tall black peak rising straight out of the water. At the foot of that peak is a cave, and in that cave, buried beneath a slab of stone, are the things you desire."

It did not take long for Perseus to find the cave. He picked up the shield and the sword, put on the sandals, and flew through the air. He circled the peak until he saw Medusa seated on the pinnacle. He knew better than to look directly at her. Instead he flew so that her body was reflected in the shield that served as a mirror. Guided by the reflection, Perseus swung his sword-like sickle in a wide arc and cut through the hideous head with a single stroke. Then he put the head in the leather pouch that Mercury had given him and flew back home.

As he flew, drops of blood from Medusa's severed head oozed through the pouch. They fell upon the Libyan sands, and every drop changed into a snake, which is why the Libyan desert has always been infested with poisonous vipers.

On his flight home Perseus was passing over the country of Ethiopia when, looking down, he beheld a group of men and women wringing their hands and lifting them in mute appeal. Descending, he found out that a young maiden was to be sacrificed.

"She is my daughter, Princess Andromeda," a woman told him. "Years ago I foolishly offended the great god Neptune. In revenge he sent a sea-monster to ravage our land, a monster as huge as a ship of war with an appetite so great that a dozen oxen barely satisfy it for a meal. No weapon can harm it. Finally, in answer to frantic prayers, Neptune promised to forgive me if I would offer my daughter to the monster. There she is, chained to a rock at the edge of the water."

Even as she spoke the hungry sea-monster, its body larger than a whale's, with two sharp horns on its head, rose from the water. Perseus soared above it, then dived on its back. The loathsome beast reared, and as it turned Perseus thrust his sword in its side. Spouting blood, the monster plunged, but before it could carry Perseus down with him, Perseus drew out the sword and sank it between the sea-beast's eyes. It was a death stroke. The monster went down in a whirlpool of boiling water, and Perseus struck the chains from Andromeda. She fainted in his arms.

Everyone cheered the deliverer. The parents fawned on him and asked him to name his reward, even if it was half the kingdom.

"I will take only this small part of your kingdom," said Perseus, holding Andromeda. "And she shall be my reward."

"Stay with us," said the queen mother. "You shall be kin to us, a favored son, captain of the army, and, later, you shall rule."

"I am not ungrateful," said Perseus. "But I have something that needs to be done in another kingdom."

Taking Andromeda with him, Perseus returned to his own country. The king was waiting. "As I expected," he sneered. "You have come back empty-handed."

"Not quite," said Perseus. "I have done as you requested. This leather pouch will prove it."

"You are not only self-important, but impudent," said the king. "That calls for extra punishment. First, however, let us see what you have in that precious bag."

Perseus opened the leather pouch and drew out the head of Medusa. Even in death the eyes were open; its glance was still deadly. Hypnotized with horror, the king stared at the dread face and, unable to avert his gaze, stiffened into stone.

CADMUS

...*The Dragon's Teeth*

T HE PRINCESS Europa had been carried off by Zeus disguised as a white bull. Her brother Cadmus was sent in search of her, but the god had taken her far away to a continent which he named after her. Cadmus could find no trace of his sister and, ashamed to return without her, he resolved to live elsewhere. Not knowing where to go, he journeyed to Delphi to consult Apollo. Usually the oracle at Delphi gave mysterious replies, but this time Apollo spoke directly to the youth.

"Do not waste your time trying to track down a bull that never can be found, especially a bull that does not happen to be a bull. You would do much better following a cow. There is, in fact, a certain cow standing in the pasture outside this shrine. Follow her. Where she lies down to rest is the place for you. There you will build a great city. It will be *your* city, and you will call it Thebes."

When he left the shrine Cadmus saw the cow. It seemed to be waiting for him. It raised its head, lowed gently, and walked slowly toward the sunset. Cadmus followed, wading fords, crossing plains, walking over hillocks, until he came to a wide meadow. There the cow lay down, looked straight at Cadmus, and once more lowed softly.

"Thank you, good creature, for guiding me to this place," said Cadmus. "Apollo should be thanked, too. Fortunately there is a spring close by. I can offer a libation of pure water with my thanks."

The spring issued from a rocky glade and as soon as Cadmus dipped his hand in the water, a monster emerged from behind the rocks. Its body was the body of a dragon, its neck was that of a thick serpent, its horrid head had a crest of flame, and its three

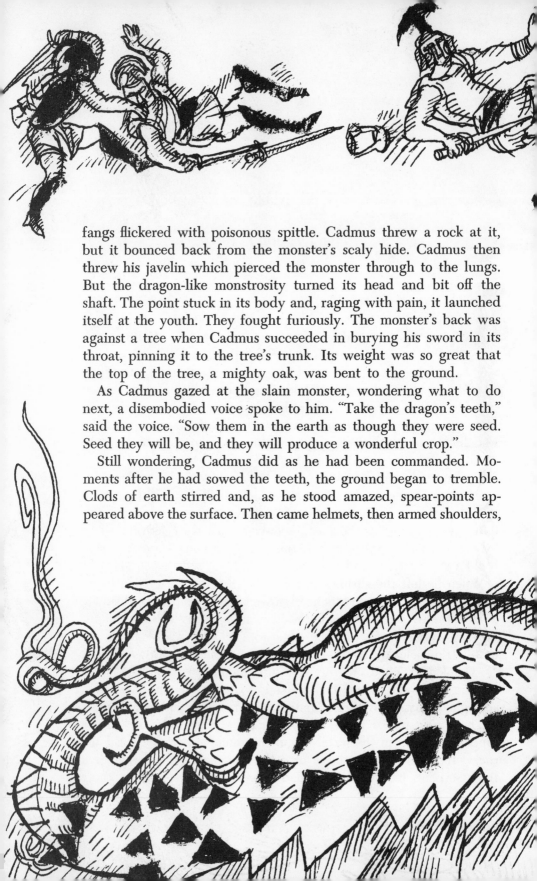

fangs flickered with poisonous spittle. Cadmus threw a rock at it, but it bounced back from the monster's scaly hide. Cadmus then threw his javelin which pierced the monster through to the lungs. But the dragon-like monstrosity turned its head and bit off the shaft. The point stuck in its body and, raging with pain, it launched itself at the youth. They fought furiously. The monster's back was against a tree when Cadmus succeeded in burying his sword in its throat, pinning it to the tree's trunk. Its weight was so great that the top of the tree, a mighty oak, was bent to the ground.

As Cadmus gazed at the slain monster, wondering what to do next, a disembodied voice spoke to him. "Take the dragon's teeth," said the voice. "Sow them in the earth as though they were seed. Seed they will be, and they will produce a wonderful crop."

Still wondering, Cadmus did as he had been commanded. Moments after he had sowed the teeth, the ground began to tremble. Clods of earth stirred and, as he stood amazed, spear-points appeared above the surface. Then came helmets, then armed shoulders,

shields, breastplates, swords, until fully armed soldiers stood before him.

"What a harvest!" cried Cadmus. "Will they be friends or foes?"

Before he could find out, one of the soldiers warned him. "Stand back!" the warrior cried. "Do not interfere! This is a long-standing feud between brothers."

Even as he spoke he hurled a lance against one of the warriors, and he himself was pierced with the other's arrow. It was as if a signal had been sounded. Man was pitted against man in furious battle. Swords clashed; warriors fell; the earth was soaked in blood. There were only five left when one of the survivors cried, "Stop! What are we doing! Brother killing his brother! We should not die but live—and live in peace."

The five stood shoulder to shoulder. Then the unseen god spoke again.

"These are the champions, the chosen few. They are worth more than an army, for they are creators, not destroyers. Peace-lovers, they look to the future. They and you will build great things together. Go now and build your city."

With the help of the chosen five, Cadmus built the city of Thebes. He ruled over it wisely—it was he who discovered the alphabet and taught the people how to use it. His wife Harmonia, daughter of the god Ares and the goddess Aphrodite, gave him five children and lived up to her name. All was harmony between them, and when they died, the gods brought them to Elysium so they could continue their good life.

BAUCIS AND PHILEMON

... The Reward of Hospitality

AUCIS and Philemon were the oldest couple in all Phrygia. They were also the poorest. Philemon had once been a farmer, always ready to help his neighbors, and Baucis had once been a lovely woman. But the farm had failed, hard times followed, age had weakened husband and wife, and they were reduced to living in a one-room cottage badly in need of repair.

One day two strangers appeared at their door. The older man spoke.

"My son and I have been traveling on foot for some time. We have knocked at many a house asking for a place to rest and a bite of food to refresh ourselves. No one offered to take us in. On the contrary, people looked scornfully at such poor wayfarers, and we were told to be on our way."

"As you can see," said Philemon, "we, too, are poor. But whatever we have we are glad to share. My wife and I welcome you. Come in and rest yourselves while we find something to eat."

Baucis brought over a bench for the strangers. One leg was broken, but she propped up the bench, fanned the embers on the hearth, threw a few pieces of dry bark to feed the flames, and hung a pot above the fire. Philemon brought in a cabbage and some greens, took down a piece of bacon that hung in the chimney, added a few onions, and the pot began to boil. A bowl of warm water was set before the strangers so that they might wash. Baucis rubbed the table with fragment thyme and covered it with a worn but still handsome cloth, a relic of better days.

"It isn't much of a stew," said Philemon, "but a few radishes and

95

olives go with it, and afterward there will be a little honey and
some wild apples."

"But our guests must be thirsty," said Baucis, as the visitors came
to the table. "There's still a little wine on the shelf."

The wine was thin and somewhat sour, but the guests did not
complain. They drank heartily, praised the food, and talked as
enthusiastically as though they were being royally entertained.
Then Philemon noticed a strange thing. No matter how much wine
was drunk, the pitcher was never empty; it seemed to fill itself.
Philemon did not know what to think or what to say. He decided
to do something to divert the attention of his guests.

"It has been a scant meal," he said. "But if you will be patient we can make amends. There is a goose—it is not young and it won't be too tender—but it should furnish us a dinner."

First, however, Philemon had to catch the goose. The bird may have been old, but Philemon was older. Every time Philemon bent to seize it, the goose honked wildly and eluded him. Philemon tried again and again, pursuing it until he was out of breath and the goose, gasping and squawking, ran for shelter between the laughing guests.

Then the older of the wayfarers spoke. "Spare your goose. You have not only housed and fed us, but you have also entertained us. For all this we are grateful. Know, then, we are gods. Weary of Olympus, we—my son Mercury and I—came disguised to earth to learn what people are like. You are the only couple in Phrygia that showed us hospitality, and you are the ones who could afford it least. The gods are not unmindful. Look!"

Jupiter waved his hand and the walls of the wooden hut changed into pure marble. Stone pillars supported a roof that was crowned with a dome of gold. The chimney widened, grew higher, and turned into a steeple with a spire. Bronze doors, carved with a hundred figures, opened to show the interior of a magnificent temple.

"Tell us your desire," said Jupiter, "and your wish shall be granted."

Philemon whispered to Baucis who had fallen on her knees. She nodded her head and Philemon, bowing, said, "We have only one desire. It is to be your priests, to serve the gods together in this temple, and to live and die together."

"It is a good wish," said Jupiter, "and it is granted. You two shall never be parted, and when the time comes for your departure from earth you will go together."

So it came to pass—except that Philemon and Baucis never really left the earth. One day, as they were exchanging memories of their long, hard, but happy life, the two very old people began to change. They were standing in front of the temple when Philemon noticed that leaves were appearing on Baucis' head, and Baucis saw that Philemon's arms were turning into branches. Bark covered their bodies; they were rooted to the ground. Their boughs intertwined.

Time was kind to them. The two trees, a graceful linden and a lordly oak, still stand there, still side by side.

POMONA

... *The Tree and the Vine*

THER girls enjoyed dancing and romancing, but Pomona delighted in only one thing: gardening. It was not only her pastime but her passion. While other girls looked forward to merry-making and the company of men, Pomona made plans for a new border of lilies, or a more formal arrangement of roses, or a ground cover of blue myrtle. Other girls were restless, longing to travel, to explore unfamiliar places. Pomona never wanted to stir from her shrubs and flowers. Her garden was her home, and she was happiest when she had a trowel or a pruning-knife in her hand.

Many suitors tried to lure her away, but she turned her back on them. She wanted to live alone and be let alone. One wooer, however, was more persistent than the rest. Vertumnus was determined that she was the woman for him and that he was definitely the man for her. When she refused to listen to him, he did not despair. He decided to disguise himself, to assume whatever character would be the one most likely to appeal to her.

Knowing Pomona's love for growing things, he presented himself to her as a farmer and brought baskets of fresh vegetables and fruit. She accepted the gifts, smiled, and went on watering her plants. He came to her as a shepherd accompanied by a small flock of sheep. She listened to his talk about feeding and shearing, patted the lambkins, and turned to clip the hedge that had grown straggly. He dressed himself as a soldier returned from war, looking for a place in which to settle down, make a living, and get married. She gave him good advice about the cultivation of land, when to put

in seedlings, and what crops would do best in this region. But she did not encourage him to speak about personal affairs.

Vertumnus kept on trying without success. Finally he disguised himself as an old country woman, a busy-body, a bearer of tittle-tattle. No woman can resist a bit of gossip, so Pomona gave ear as the old woman spoke about the poor quality of this year's fruit, the failure of other gardeners to grow specimen pansies and peonies, and the unquestioned superiority of Pomona's own garden.

"Nothing I've seen equals what you have done, my dear," said the disguised Vertumnus. "Everyone says there is only one thing more beautiful than your garden, and that is you."

"You flatter me," said Pomona.

"Not in the least. To be honest, there is just one person whose craft can compare with yours. He is a countryman called Vertumnus. I hear that, although he is well-liked and he can make things blossom that never bloomed before, he is strangely sad. He makes no secret of the fact that he adores you but that you treat him coldly. He says he cannot understand how you, who have such love for everything in nature, can be so cruel, so cold-hearted, when it comes to human nature."

"I remember the young man," said Pomona. "Of all the men who plagued me, I found him the least objectionable. In fact he seemed quite pleasant and rather well-favored. But he was a man—and what good is a man?"

"Let me tell you a fable," said Vertumnus. "Once upon a time there was an elm. It was a sturdy tree, but it stood alone and it was lonely. Not far from where it grew, there was a vine, as lovely as the elm was lordly. But, without support, it trailed on the ground. The vine needed something to cling to; the elm wanted to feel that its strength was of use. The lesson is plain. Tree and vine needed each other, just as"—he straightened up and cast off the disguise— "I need you and you need me."

Pomona gasped, too startled to speak. Wide-eyed, she stared at the sturdy figure who stood before her. Then she laughed.

"I should have seen through your disguise—all your disguises," she said. "You are a clever story-teller, Vertumnus. You are also a good teacher. What is more, you are a powerful persuader."

And Pomona lifted her face to be kissed.

PYRAMUS AND THISBE

...The Mulberry Tree

ABYLON was the home of two unhappy lovers who lived next door to each other. They were unhappy because their parents refused to let them marry, had even forbidden them to meet. But Pyramus and the lovely Thisbe found a way of telling each other how deeply they felt and how much they needed to be together. They had discovered a crack in the wall which separated their dwellings and through this crack they could talk and even exchange kisses. It was not a satisfactory love-making, but it was the best they could do—at least for a while.

One morning Pyramus revolted. "We are acting like children," he whispered fiercely through the wall. "We have a right to live and love. Since our parents continue to treat us as though we were infants, we should do as we think best. Would you dare leave home?"

"I would do whatever you say," answered Thisbe. "Your will is my will; your desire is mine."

"Then listen," said Pyramus. "Tonight when it grows dark, slip out of the house and follow the city wall. It will be a cloudy night, but there will be enough moonlight for you to make your way to the little grove that surrounds the tomb of Ninus. I will meet you at the foot of the mulberry tree that grows there. Whoever arrives first will wait for the other."

"I know I will be there first," said Thisbe. "I cannot wait for the sun to set."

True to her word, Thisbe was the first to arrive. She found the mulberry tree with its white fruit, but as soon as she sat down she saw that the bushes were violently agitated by some prowling

animal. It was a lion covered with the blood of the creature it had
slain, and it was coming to drink at a nearby spring. Not knowing
that the lion was merely thirsty, Thisbe was terrified and, dropping her cloak in panic, ran and hid in the deepest part of the grove.
The lion had no intention of pursuing her, but, seeing Thisbe's
cloak, picked it up, tossed and tore it with its bloody jaws. Then,
slaking its thirst, it slunk away.

A few minutes later Pyramus came to the spot and saw, instead
of Thisbe, Thisbe's torn cloak. There was only one explanation for
Thisbe's absence and the blood-soaked garment: some savage beast
must have devoured her. Wild-eyed, Pyramus beat his breast and
cried desperately.

"It is all my fault!" he moaned. "It was I who suggested the plan.

It was I who arranged a meeting in this perilous place. Life without Thisbe is unthinkable!"

He took up the cloak, covered it with tears and kisses, and carried it to the tree. "It was here that we should have met, and since we cannot live together, it is here that I will die." Drawing his sword he thrust it into his heart. As the blood spurted, it stained the white mulberries.

It was quiet when Thisbe timidly emerged from her hiding place. She was still trembling, not sure whether she was safe and even more uncertain when she noticed that the mulberries were not white but red. Then she saw a body at the foot of the tree and realized it was Pyramus. She screamed and sank to the ground beside him.

"O my love," she wailed. "Who has done this thing? Answer me! It is your Thisbe crying to you! Lift up your head! Speak to me!"

Hearing her voice, Pyramus struggled to raise himself and take her in his arms. But it was too late. His eyes closed and he fell back upon the ground.

"Dead!" cried Thisbe disconsolately. "Then I will die, too." Taking up the sword in both hands she buried it in her breast. Her blood mingled with that of Pyramus. It seeped to the roots of the tree, flowed up the trunk, spread through the branches, and colored the fruit.

Ever since then mulberries have been dark red.

JULIUS CAESAR

... *The Ides of March*

N HIS mid-fifties Julius Caesar was at the height of his glory. As a warrior he was adored by his soldiers. As a general he had won victory after victory. He had driven back two tribes of German invaders across the Rhine. He had spent nine years fighting in Gaul until all western Europe was subject to Rome. He had extended Roman rule by invading Britain and establishing an army there. He had crossed the Rubicon and was master of all Italy.

As a ruler he was beloved by the people. He never tired of doing things for them. He spent much of his income on festivals and food for the hungry. In return, the citizens offered him the crown. When he refused it, they named him "Father of his Country" and made him dictator for life. He was literally idolized. Statues of Caesar were placed in temples; his face appeared on all sorts of coins; the seventh month of the year was called Julius (or July) in his honor.

He was, in short, worshiped by everyone except the politicians. They feared and envied him. Cassius was the most evil-minded of these. He was wildly jealous of Caesar. They had been schoolmates, and he had always considered himself Caesar's equal if not his superior. Now things were different. He complained (in Shakespeare's words): "This man is now become a god, and Cassius is a wretched creature and must bend his body if Caesar carelessly but nod at him."

Cassius organized a conspiracy. He knew that he could not show personal hatred; there had to be a cause. He had little trouble convincing several others that Caesar was a tyrant and that, for the

good of Rome, they would have to get rid of him. Hardest to convince was Caesar's friend, Brutus. Brutus was a noble being, an idealist, a dedicated lover of Rome. He found it difficult to hate. Yet he, a loyal citizen, a believer in democracy, hated dictatorship. What Cassius suggested—nothing less than Caesar's assassination—was abhorrent to him. Deeply troubled, he could not sleep. Finally he came to an unhappy decision. He decided that it would be better to destroy a despot than let a despot destroy the government. Caesar was his friend, but friendship must not stand in the way of saving Rome from tyranny. He remembered what Cassius had said:

> "Why, man, he doth bestride the narrow world
> Like a Colossus, and we petty men
> Walk under his huge legs."

Caesar was unaware of any conspiracy. One morning, as he was walking, attended by a devoted crowd, a soothsayer, who foretold the future, warned him. "Caesar!" he called. "Beware the ides of March!"

Caesar shrugged. "He is a dreamer. Why should the fifteenth of March disturb me more than any other day? Let us leave him—pass."

A few weeks later Caesar was on his way to the Capitol. Passing the soothsayer he could not help but tease him. "Today is the fifteenth," he said. "The ides of March have come."

"So they have," softly answered the soothsayer. "But they are not yet past."

Caesar smiled, but inwardly he was troubled. The night before, there had been a violent storm and his wife had waked in terror.

"It is not the storm that woke me," she told Caesar, trembling. "It was a dream, a terrible dream. I dreamed that lightning had struck the house, that the roof had caved in, and that—I can see it still!—you had been slain and were lying in my arms. Do not leave me. Do not, I beg you, go out of doors today."

Caesar shook his head. "Do not let a dream alarm you. My time has not yet come, and when it comes I will meet it without fear.

"Cowards die many times before their deaths,
The valiant never taste of death but once."

Not to be deterred, Caesar went to the Capitol. He was stopped on the way by Artemidorus, a teacher, who knew some of Cassius' confederates and had found out their plan. He handed Caesar a roll of paper.

"Read it," said Artemidorus. "Read it at once. It concerns you greatly."

Caesar took the paper, but thinking it was merely an appeal for aid, did not unroll it. So many people thronged to shake his hand or wish him well that he never had a chance to see what was written. Had he glanced at even the first line his life would have been saved.

When he entered the Capitol, the entire Senate stood up to honor him. As he seated himself, many flocked about him, including the conspirators. One of them presented a petition for the return of a brother who had been banished from Rome. When Caesar refused, they pressed closer, and suddenly Caesar was struck on the shoulder. This was the signal. Before he could stand, the conspirators drew their daggers and stabbed Caesar again and again. He did not succumb until he saw his friend Brutus with a bloody weapon in his hand.

"And you, too, Brutus?" he said. "Then fall, Caesar."

With these words he died.

DAVID AND GOLIATH

... The Shepherd Boy and the Giant

APART from its religious grandeur, the Bible is one of the greatest of all works of literature. It is a priceless collection of stories, poems, parables, prophecies, and legends. It is the history of a people and reflects the thoughts of people everywhere. The poet Heinrich Heine said that it embodies the whole drama of humanity.

Among the thrilling stories, one of the most dramatic is the tale of David, the shepherd boy, and his encounter with the champion warrior of the Philistines.

David was the youngest son of a farmer. His older brothers had gone to be soldiers and David was left to tend the sheep and goats that grazed on his father's pastures. He was a handsome youth, "ruddy, and withal of a beautiful countenance, goodly to look upon."

Besides being a shepherd, David was a music-maker. When King Saul was threatened by the Philistines and troubled by unhappy thoughts, one of his servants sent for the boy David to play before the king. David brought his harp and played until the music brought consolation to Saul "and the evil spirits departed from him." The king was so pleased with the boy that he made David his armor-bearer.

But Saul was still worried by the enemy who had declared war on Israel. The time for a final decision was at hand. The Philistines and the Israelites faced each other on opposite mountains. The leader of the Philistines was Goliath of Gath, a giant of ten feet high. He was a frightening figure not only because of his brute strength but also because of his mighty armor. He wore a helmet of heavy brass, a coat of steel mesh, plates of reinforced metal on his legs, and he carried an iron spear that weighed twenty pounds. He came out from the Philistine ranks, stood before the Israelites, and taunted them.

"You are a puny lot to think of battling. Choose a man and let him come to me. If he be able to fight and kill me, then the Philistines will be your servants. But if I prevail and kill him, then shall you serve us."

When Saul heard these words he and all Israel were dismayed and knew not what to do.

Meanwhile David had returned to the farm to help his aged father. Three of David's older brothers were with the army. His father called his youngest son and said, "Take this basket of food to your brothers—there's bread and cheese and other provisions—and tell me how they fare."

David arrived just as Goliath shouted his mocking challenge. He had jeered at the Israelites many times, but no one had answered. David was shocked. "Why are you afraid?" he asked. "He may be big, but he is only a man. I will fight him."

When King Saul heard of this, he argued with David. "You are brave, but you are only a shepherd boy. This Philistine has been a man of war from his youth."

"Once when I was taking care of the sheep," said David, "there

came a lion and took a lamb from the flock. I went after him and seized the lion by his hair; I grappled with him, slew the lion, and saved the lamb. If I could face a lion, surely I should not fear a Philistine who dares defy the army of the Lord."

Saul put his hand on David's shoulder. "You are resolute," he said. "I will not stop you. Go, and the Lord go with you."

David was about to leave, but Saul motioned him to stay. "Let me arm you properly," he said. "At least you should be as well equipped as the giant."

He put his own helmet on David's head, girded him with his own coat of mail, and placed his own sword in his hand.

David thanked him, but as soon as he was outside, he removed the armor to which he was not accustomed and which only hampered him. He took his shepherd's crook, a thing he knew how to use, and looked for something else with which he was familiar. He picked five smooth stones from a brook, put them in his shepherd's bag, and tested his sling. Then he called to Goliath. "Where is the braggart of Gath?"

Goliath came forth, saw the unarmed boy with nothing but a shepherd's crook, and sneered. "Do you think I am a dog that you come at me with a stick?"

When David did not answer, Goliath grew furious. "Come a little nearer and I will give your flesh to the fowls of the air and to the beasts of the field!"

David replied. "You come with a sword and a spear. But I come in the name of the Lord of hosts, the God of the army of Israel. The Lord will deliver you into my hand, and it will be your flesh, not mine, that will feed the fowls of the air and the beasts of the field. And all the earth will know that there is a God in Israel."

Goliath took a huge step forward. As he advanced, David put his hand in the shepherd's bag and took out a smooth stone. He fitted it into the sling and hurled the stone at the oncoming giant. It hit the Philistine and sunk deep into his forehead and he fell upon his face.

The Israelites shouted with joy. "His head! His head!" they cried. David sprang forward and, since he had no sword of his own, he drew Goliath's sword from its sheath, and cut off the giant's head.

When the Philistines saw that their champion had been killed by an unarmed boy, they felt they were witnessing something miraculous. They threw down their arms and fled. And Israel once more was at peace.

SHADRACH, MESHACH, AND ABEDNEGO

... *The Fiery Furnace*

NEBUCHADNEZZAR was a mighty king who ruled Assyria six hundred years before the Christian era. He built the world-famous Hanging Gardens and rebuilt Babylon, which celebrated the heathen god Baal. He conquered Jerusalem and compelled the Jews to slave for him and worship his idols.

He was proudest of a huge image his sculptors had made for him. It was ninety feet high and nine feet wide and was solid gold. For its dedication he summoned princes, governors, judges, captains, councilors, treasurers, and all the rulers of the provinces. When they were gathered together, a herald cried out: "It is commanded, O people, that when you hear the sound of cornet, flute, harp, psaltery, sackbut, and all kinds of music you shall fall down and worship the golden image which the king has set up. And whoso faileth to fall down and worship, he shall be cast into the midst of a burning fiery furnace."

Accordingly, when the people heard the sound of cornet, flute, harp, psaltery, sackbut, and all kinds of music, they fell down and worshiped the golden image which the king had set up.

However, word came to the king that there were three who had disobeyed his command. They were three Jews, and their names were Shadrach, Meshach, and Abednego. Nebuchadnezzar was furious. Raging, he gave orders to bring the three men in. When they stood before him, he spoke.

"Is it true that you do not serve my gods? And is it true that you refuse to worship the golden image which I have set up? You do not deserve it, but you shall have another chance. When you hear the sound of cornet, flute, harp, psaltery, sackbut, and all kinds of music, you shall fall down and worship. But if you do not, in the same hour you shall be cast into a burning fiery furnace. Who is your God that can deliver you out of my hands? Answer me!"

Shadrach, Meshach, and Abednego replied: "O Nebuchadnezzar, we can answer you. If it be his will, our God will deliver us out of the burning fiery furnace and out of your hands. But if not, we still will not serve your gods nor worship the golden image which you have set up."

Wild with anger, Nebuchadnezzar commanded that the furnace be heated seven times hotter than usual, that Shadrach, Meshach, and Abednego should be bound, and they should then be cast into the burning fiery furnace. When the three were bound and brought before the furnace, the flames were so fierce that the men who led Shadrach, Meshach, and Abednego were burned to death. But Shadrach, Meshach, and Abednego did not flinch. They walked straight into the burning fiery furnace. There they prayed and glorified their God. Their prayers were long and confident. They ended with this exaltation:

> "O give thanks unto the Lord because he is gracious:
> For his mercy endureth forever.
> O all ye that worship the Lord, bless the God of gods;
> Praise him and give him thanks:
> For his mercy endureth forever."

When he heard that the three men were still alive, Nebuchadnezzar questioned his councilors. "Did I not order that those three be bound and cast into the midst of the fire?"

"True, O king," they replied.

"I have looked into the burning fiery furnace and I saw not three men but four. They were all walking through the flames unhurt, and the fourth looked like the messenger of a god, an angel."

Nebuchadnezzar came near the mouth of the burning fiery furnace, and he said: "Shadrach, Meshach, and Abednego, come forth. Come here and let me see you, for you are truly servants of a most high God."

Shadrach, Meshach, and Abednego came out from the midst of the fire. And the princes, governors, judges, captains, councilors, treasurers, and all the rulers of the provinces could see that the fire had no power over them. Not a hair of their heads was singed;

their clothes were not harmed; nor was there the smallest smell of burning about them.

Then Nebuchadnezzar spoke again: "Blessed be the God of Shadrach, Meshach, and Abednego. He has sent his angel and saved his servants who trusted in him. These men defied the king's word and yielded their bodies rather than worship any god but their own God. Therefore I make this decree: that every people, nation, and language which speak anything against the God of Shadrach, Meshach, and Abednego shall be cut in pieces and their houses be made into a dunghill. Because there is no other God who could accomplish what we have seen."

Then Nebuchadnezzar promoted Shadrach, Meshach, and Abednego to important positions in the province of Babylon. There they lived a long time, held in awe by many and honored by all.

ESTHER

...Who Saved Her People

AHASUERUS, king of the Medes and the Persians, loved pomp and elegance. His palace at Shushan shone with gem-like brilliance. The curtains were green, the wall hangings were blue, and the ivory-white drapes were fastened with purple cords. The couches were silver, the beds were gold, and the floors were inlaid with designs of red, blue, white, and black marble.

In the third year of his reign Ahasuerus made a great feast and invited the princes and other nobles of the hundred and twenty provinces he controlled. The festivities lasted for one hundred and eighty days. On the seventh day, when everyone was praising the splendors, the king, made foolish by wine, wanted to display another of his treasures: Vashti, his radiant queen. But Vashti refused to be exhibited. Embarrassed in front of his guests, Ahasuerus was angered and asked his councilors what should be done to a disobedient wife.

"She has not only dishonored the king," said his chief councilor, "but she has also dishonored the princes and nobles and all the people that are in the provinces of the king. Moreover, she has set a bad example. If it becomes known that the queen will not obey her lord, the king, then all other women will stop obeying their husbands. Therefore, Vashti should be deposed. She should give up her position of royalty and her place should be taken by someone worthier."

This verdict pleased the king. He ordered officers in all his provinces to select the loveliest of girls and bring them to his court. The one who pleased Ahasuerus most would be queen instead of Vashti.

Among the king's servants was a Jew named Mordecai who had been brought to the palace along with others when the Persians captured Jerusalem. He had raised his beautiful cousin Hadassah, called Esther, who had no father or mother, as his own daughter. When Esther was brought before the king, Ahasuerus immediately fell in love with her. He divorced Vashti and set the royal crown on Esther's head. Acting on Mordecai's caution, Esther did not reveal her background or her kin.

Coming and going through the palace, Mordecai learned of a plot against the king's life. He told Esther and Esther told the king. At first Ahasuerus refused to believe it, but when it was found to be true, the conspirators were hanged.

"Make a record of this," Ahasuerus said to his scribe. "It is something not to be forgotten. Nor must we forget who exposed the plot."

When it came time to appoint a new grand vizier, Ahasuerus chose a councilor named Haman. Haman had always been proud of himself, but now his self-importance surpassed all bounds. He decreed that all the king's servants should bow down to him. Mordecai refused and was summoned to appear before a stony-faced Haman.

"Why do you not bow and give me reverence as you are supposed to do?" asked Haman angrily.

"Because," said Mordecai, "I do not lower my head to any man. I am a Jew and I bow only to God."

"You shall be punished for your impudence," said Haman. "Moreover, I shall punish not only you but also your race. Your people will feel my wrath!"

Haman then went to Ahasuerus and complained. "There is a certain people scattered among your provinces who are different from us," he said. "They make their own laws and refuse to obey ours. A rebellious lot, they are an ever-present danger."

Ahasuerus was troubled. "Our laws must be upheld," he said. "What should be done?"

"May it please the king to make a law that these lawless people should be destroyed, and that I will pay ten thousand talents of silver when we are rid of those people."

"It shall be as you say," said the king. "Do as you think best."

When he heard what had happened, Mordecai mourned. He put on sackcloth and ashes and all the Jews wept and wailed. Esther mourned with them, but she told Mordecai she would try to think of a way to help.

"The king," she said, "has withdrawn in a somber mood. I have not seen him in thirty days. It is said that anyone who attempts to see him without being summoned is put to death. Only if the king holds out the golden scepter is one permitted to live. I still hope to see him and speak with him."

"Be careful," said Mordecai. "If you say nothing, perhaps deliverance will come to the Jews from some other quarter. If you speak you may be destroyed. But perhaps you have been chosen to play a part at just such a time as this."

"I know now what I have to do," said Esther. "Tell all the Jews to fast and pray for three days and nights. My maidens and I will also fast and pray. Then I will go to the king without being summoned. And if I perish, I perish."

On the third day Esther put on her royal apparel and appeared before the king without being summoned. When Ahasuerus saw her loveliness and the sad expression on her face, he was deeply moved. He stretched out the golden scepter and Esther touched its tip.

"What will you have, my beauteous queen?" he said. "Name it and you shall have it, even to half of my kingdom."

"It is no great thing," replied Esther. "But if it seems good to you, let the king and Haman come this day to the banquet I have prepared."

When Haman received word he made haste to join the king. And, in the midst of the banquet, Ahasuerus again asked Esther if she had any request to make, and Esther replied that she would be happy if the king and Haman would come again tomorrow. The king smiled his assent.

Haman was overjoyed. He ran home and told everyone that he had been honored above all the princes and nobles in the kingdom. "Yes," he said smugly, "the queen invited no one but the king and myself. And I am invited to be with them again tomorrow."

The next day, however, Haman's self-satisfaction gave way to fury when Mordecai failed to bow down to him as he came through the courtyard of the palace. He ordered a gallows to be built. On it he would hang Mordecai.

The king had not slept and, since he remained wide awake, he commanded that the book of records be read to him. When it came to the part about the conspiracy against him which Mordecai had discovered, he said, "What honor and reward were bestowed upon my servant Mordecai for this?"

"Nothing, your majesty," replied the scribe.

In the morning Ahasuerus summoned Haman. "I have a question for you," he said. "What should be done for a man whom the king has determined to honor?"

Thinking that he was the man whom the king had determined to give new honors, Haman replied, "For the man whom the king delights to honor, royal robes should be brought, the same which the king has worn, and let him be given the horse that the king rides, and let a crown be set upon his head. Let one of the highest nobles place the robe and the crown on the man and let him be led on horseback through the streets of the city and let it be proclaimed to all that this is the man whom the king delights to honor."

Then the king said to Haman, "You are right. Hurry, then, and take the robe and the crown and the horse to the man who is sitting in the courtyard in sackcloth and ashes, my servant, Mordecai the Jew."

The king's order had to be obeyed. Having done what had been commanded, Haman went home and hid in shame. Then he remembered the banquet and was somewhat cheered.

At the banquet Ahasuerus again asked Esther to name her request. This time she answered gravely.

"If I have found favor in your sight, O king," she said, "let my life and the lives of my people be spared. For we are to be destroyed. All of us are to be slain."

"Who is he and where is he," said the king, frowning, "who has it in his heart to do such a thing?"

"He sits here," said Esther. "The man who planned this is the enemy, Haman."

Seeing the king's anger, one of the servants dared to speak up. "Your majesty, there is a gallows which Haman had made for Mordecai. What should be done with it?"

"Hang Haman on it," said the king.

When that was done, Mordecai was called before the king, and the king placed the royal ring on Mordecai's finger. And all the Jews were full of light and gladness and joy. And they made a feast, a feast called Purim, which still celebrates the great day when Esther saved her people.

ODIN

... The Price of Wisdom

THE NORSEMEN made gods in their own image, strong and savage, but with a grim sense of humor. Unlike the Greek gods, the gods of the North were not immortal. Nor were they invincible. On the contrary, they were constantly at war with enemies who sometimes overcame them. Their myths took on the character of the Norse countries, a region of towering cliffs and deep fjords, with a coastline lashed by polar seas and skies pierced by icy stars.

The chief god was Odin, sometimes spelled Oithin, Wotan, and Woden, who gave the name of Wodensday (Wednesday) to the fourth day of the week. He was also known as "Sky-ruler" and "All-father." Besides being the most powerful of the gods, Odin was also the most contemplative. He received information every day from his two ravens, called Thought and Memory, which flew all over the world. Although Odin knew what had happened, he had only a foreboding of what was to come. It troubled him. He had knowledge, but he needed wisdom.

Odin determined to visit Ymir who guarded the hidden Well of Wisdom. He had to pass through Jotunheim, the stronghold of the giants, and Niflheim, the country of darkness and death from which there is no return. Odin put on a cloak made of the blue of the sky and he was as invisible as air. He remained invisible when he stood before Ymir.

"One who drinks daily from the Well of Wisdom is not deceived by a cloak," said Ymir. "I see you. You are Odin, the Sky-ruler, and you have come to ask a favor."

"Since you are wisdom itself," said Odin, "you must know what favor I have come to ask."

"You wish to do what neither god nor man may do—except at a price. You wish to drink from my well."

"You are right," said Odin. "What is the price?"

"Your right eye," said Ymir.

Odin did not speak. But as he towered above Ymir, lightning flashed and thunder rolled ominously.

Ymir did not move. Nor did he seem at all frightened. "The All-father may control the elements," he said, "but he cannot destroy wisdom."

"Again you are right," said Odin. "It is a terrible price you demand, but I will pay it."

"Drink then," said Ymir, and handed him a horn that reached through the well into the roots of the earth.

Odin drank, drank deeply. He saw what was to come. He saw all that would afflict men and gods with woes and wars, with fears and hatreds, with unthinkable tyrannies and threats of total destruction. And he also saw that the one thing which could save men as well as gods was wisdom.

Odin put down the horn and gave Ymir his right eye. "It was a terrible price," he said, "but I am content. Wisdom is worth whatever must be paid for it."

THOR

...How the Thunderer Was Tricked

STRONGEST and most hot tempered of the Norse gods was Odin's eldest son, Thor, the thunderer. Nothing could withstand the blows of his hammer which, after it was thrown, returned to his hand. Enemies fled in panic when it whistled through the air; ship-wrecking storms sprang up in its wake. Yet Thor was as much honored as feared. It was Thor for whom the fifth day of the week was named: Thursday.

The giants were the chief enemies of the gods. Thor boasted that he could not only outfight but outwit the greatest and wiliest giant ever born. To prove it he started out for Jotunheim, the land of the giants, accompanied by his younger brother, Loki, and his servant, Thialfi, who carried the provisions.

At nightfall they came to what seemed to be a deserted house and camped in one of its five huge rooms. They did not sleep well, for the earth shook continually and there were noises that sounded like earthquakes. When they wakened and went out, they saw a giant lying on the ground and realized that what they thought was the rumbling of earthquakes was merely the giant's snoring. Thor was about to use his hammer when the giant awoke.

"I know who you are," said the giant, yawning. "The hammer tells me. You are Thor, the thunderer. My name is Skrymir, and I see you have taken advantage of my hospitality without asking for it."

"What hospitality?" asked Thor.

"I didn't mean to mention it," said Skrymir. "But you spent the night in my glove, in the thumb, to be exact. May I ask where you are going?"

"To Jotunheim," said Thor. "Not for war but for a test of superiority."

"You will find my cousins friendly enough," said Skrymir. "They love games and contests of wit. The way to Jotunheim is long and confusing. I'll be happy to guide you part of the way. First, let us put all our provisions in one bag. I'll tie up the bag and carry it over my shoulder."

After they had traveled most of the day, Skrymir lay down to sleep. Thor was hungry and started to untie the bag containing food. However, Skrymir had knotted it so tightly that Thor could not loosen a single knot. Hot-headed Thor lost his temper and struck the sleeping Skrymir with his mighty hammer.

Skrymir woke. "An acorn must have fallen on my head," he said. "Anyway I have had enough sleep, and I must be on my way. You are not too far from your goal. Keep to the road that curves eastward and you will come to Jotunheim some time tomorrow. Let me give you a piece of advice. I am a fair-size giant, but my cousins are much bigger than I am. They are also cleverer, and they like to play tricks on little fellows like you. Be careful. Don't boast too much."

Thor and his companions were not too sorry to see him go, but they followed his directions and next day they entered Jotunheim. They stared. The houses were so huge that, although they bent so far back that their heads almost came off their shoulders, they could not see to the tops of the buildings. The enormous gates of the palace were shut, but they had no trouble passing through the bars. When they stood before the king, Utgard-Loki, the ruler laughed.

"So you are Thor," he said. "I can't believe there is much force in that little body of yours. I may be wrong. Since you came in peace, I assume you are here to show your skills. What are the feats in which you excel?"

"I don't want to boast," said Thor, "but there are many things we perform better than anyone. For example, my brother Loki can eat faster and more thoroughly than anyone in the world."

"Interesting if true," said the king of the giants. "Let us see."

A wooden platter six feet long filled with meat was brought in. Loki was placed at one end of the platter and the king's man, Logi, was placed at the other. They ate rapidly until they met in the middle. Then the king pronounced judgment.

"You will notice," he said to Thor, "that your brother ate only the flesh from the bones, whereas my man ate not only the flesh but also all the bones. Perhaps you can do better at something else. What do you suggest?"

"My servant Thialfi is the fastest runner on earth," said Thor. "He can outrace anyone matched against him."

"I, too, have someone who is considered quite a runner," said the king. "His name is Hugi. Let us go outside and watch."

Thialfi ran so fast that he seemed to fly. But Hugi covered the ground so swiftly that there was no question who would win. He was so far ahead that when he turned back at the end of the course, he met Thialfi near the start. They raced three times, and each time Hugi beat his competitor by a greater margin.

"What do you propose next?" asked the king.

"A drinking contest," said Thor. "I believe I can outdrink anyone you choose."

The king called to his cupbearer to bring in the horn from which his followers drank .

"Most of my men can empty the horn at a single draught," said the king. "A few of them take two draughts. None needs three."

Thor picked up the horn. He was thirsty and he took a long drink. However, when he set the horn down, it seemed to be filled to overflowing. He took a deep breath and gave another long pull. But the liquor had scarcely receded, although the horn could now be tilted without spilling. Once more Thor tried to empty the horn. He drank till he was out of breath and the veins stood out in his neck. But the horn was still almost full.

The king of the giants smiled. "I see you are not so thirsty nor as hearty as you are supposed to be. I doubt that you could win any of the ordinary games we play. Still, would you still like to try?"

"I will try," said Thor grimly.

"One of the more trifling games we sometimes play consists of lifting a pet cat. The children are very good at it. It is perhaps too foolish for the great god Thor, but it may amuse you."

The king snapped his fingers and a gray cat sprang into the hall. Thor rubbed the creature's head and the cat purred. Then confidently he put his right hand under the cat to pick it from the floor. The cat refused to be lifted. The more Thor strained, the more the cat arched its back and clung on the ground. Heaving and tugging, Thor was only able to get the cat to raise one of its paws.

"One more test," said Utgard-Loki, the king. "Then you may rest. What will it be?"

"You have made enough fun of me," said Thor. "You have also made me angry, ready to fight or wrestle with the strongest of your men."

"I doubt that I could persuade any of my men to wrestle with you," said the king. "You are too puny. But I will match my old nurse, Elli, against you. In her day she has thrown many a man and she still has some strength left."

Thor looked scornful as an old woman came in. He grappled with her, but she held her ground. The more he struggled to throw her, the firmer she stood. He panted and tussled, he scuffled and sweated, but it was she who brought him down to his knees.

"You have done your best," said the king. "I will say that for you. The hour is late. There is food for those who are still hungry and beds for those who would sleep. We will talk in the morning."

Next day when they were ready to depart, Utgard-Loki accompanied them to the gate and asked whether the journey to Jotunheim had been worth while.

"I am ashamed," said Thor. "And what troubles me most is your contempt. You will always consider me a braggart who had nothing to boast about."

"On the contrary," said the king of the giants. "We were afraid of you. We still are. Had I known the strength you possessed, I would never have permitted you to enter Jotunheim. You had us all in danger."

"You are joking," said Thor.

"In a way you are right," said Utgard-Loki. "I played a joke on you, but you almost turned the joke on us. You have been deceived by illusions; all the games and contests were tricks. Let me explain. First, when Loki, your brother, ate, he ate like Hunger itself, but he was no match for Logi. Logi was the spirit of Fire, and Fire consumes everything. Next your servant Thialfi ran splendidly, but how could he hope to keep pace with Hugi. Hugi was Thought, and how can anyone outrun Thought? Then there was the horn. When you attempted to empty it you did something so stupendous that, had I not seen you do it, I would never have believed it. For one end of the horn is deep in the ocean and, when you come to the shore you will notice how the sea has shrunk because of your three great draughts. Even more wonderful was what you did with the cat. My magic made it look like a cat, but it really was the Midgard serpent which is twined around the world. When you lifted one of its paws we were struck with terror, for you loosened the foundations of the earth. Your wrestling with old Elli was the most wonderful feat of all. Elli was Old Age to whom every man must yield. Yet you stood up against Old Age and held it off for a while. Yes, Thor, you are mighty, and I am glad you are going. I will do all in my power to stop you from ever coming back."

LOKI

... *The Apples of Youth*

LOKI WAS Thor's opposite. Thor was blunt and straight-forward; Loki was sharp and scheming. Thor was good-hearted and generous: Loki was mean and malicious. Of all the Norse gods, Loki was the most dangerous. At his best, he was mischievous; at his worst, he was evil. Odin was fascinated by his many moods and, somehow, seemed to enjoy his company.

One day Odin and Loki wandered over an unpopulated part of earth and were lost. For days they walked over rough ground until they were footsore and famished. At dusk they saw a few oxen feeding on thin grass.

"There is our dinner!" said Loki. Killing one of the animals, Loki built a fire, and started to roast the ox. However, the meat would not cook. Loki kept feeding the fire, but the meat remained not only raw but cold. Then, from a nearby tree, they heard a mocking laugh. Looking up they saw a giant eagle gazing at them.

"This is my territory," said the eagle. "And those are my cattle. No fire will roast them without my permission. Let me have a small share of the meat and I will let it cook."

Odin and Loki agreed, and as soon as the meat was done, the eagle swooped down, snatched most of the ox and started to fly away. Furious at being cheated, Loki seized a pole and struck at the eagle. Instead of hurting the eagle, one end of the pole stuck to its back. Worse, Loki's hands stuck to the other end. The eagle spread its wings and Loki was dragged away from Odin.

"Help!" cried Loki as the eagle soared. "Put me down! Put me down and you may have the rest of the ox!"

"I do not want the ox," said the eagle. "That was just a trick to get you in my power. I want one thing only."

"What is that?" gasped Loki.

"Iduna," said the eagle. "Iduna and her apples."

Loki was ready to faint, but he managed to breathe. "You know that is impossible. The gods would never surrender her. It is her apples that keep the gods immortal. Whenever they feel old or tired, a taste of the apples makes them young again."

"I know the magic power of those apples," said the eagle. "That is why I want them."

"But I could never steal the apples," moaned Loki. "Iduna keeps them too well guarded.

"Then steal Iduna, too. Unless you swear to get her for me, I will drop you from the highest point in the heavens and your body will be broken on the rocks."

Loki had little choice. Also, he thought to himself, he could play a trick on the gods. While they grew old, he would stay young.

"I will get Iduna for you," said the crafty schemer. "On one condition: that you will let me taste the apples from time to time."

"You have given me your oath. Get Iduna, and we will come to terms," said the eagle. Gliding down, he dropped Loki gently on a patch of grass.

When it came time to fulfill his part of the bargain, Loki had made his plan. He knew he could not kidnap Iduna where she could call on the other gods. He would have to get her alone.

"Iduna," he told her, "I know a place where there are trees full of the most wonderful apples. I dislike to say it, but the apples are even sweeter than yours."

"I cannot believe it," said Iduna. "Mine are the sweetest, the most perfect apples ever grown."

"If you will come with me, I will prove what I have said," said Loki. "You won't regret it."

"I still do not believe it," said Iduna. "But I am curious. I will bring my apples with me to compare and show how wrong you must be."

Loki led her through a dense wood to the appointed place. There was a loud whirring of wings, and before she could realize what was happening, the eagle carried off Iduna and her magic apples.

It was not long before she was missed. When the gods could not find Iduna, they grew alarmed. When time went by and there were no apples to give them eternal youth, their faces showed wrinkles, their hair turned gray, their limbs grew stiff. Terror seized the gods. Iduna must be found—and at once. But who might know where she had gone?

It was learned that she was last seen walking out of Asgard, the home of the gods, with Loki. Loki was brought before a council and, after he had been threatened with torture and expulsion, confessed what he had done.

"Unless you bring back Iduna," said Odin, "you will be maimed and flung from the heavens into the outer void."

"How am I to know where she is?" whimpered Loki.

"It is you who lost her," said Odin. "It is you who must find her."

Loki was desperate. He would have to match his wits against the power of the eagle, who he knew was a giant in disguise. He equipped himself with the wings of the swiftest falcon and flew to Jotunheim. He circled over the domain of the giants until he spied Iduna. She was alone, locked up, weeping bitterly. The falcon came down and, seeing a huge bird overhead, Iduna started to scream.

"Hush!" said Loki. "I have come to save you."

"Who are you?" asked Iduna.

"You would not trust me if I told you," said Loki. "Besides, this is not a time for questions. Get ready."

"But how can I leave here? I am locked in."

"I will change you into a nut and carry you easily."

"But the apples! Can you take them, too?"

"I would not dare go back to Asgard without them," said Loki.

Carrying Iduna in the shape of a nut in one claw and her basket of apples in the other, Loki flew off just as the giant eagle returned and, missing Iduna, started immediately in pursuit. More powerful than the fastest falcon, he gained on Loki who was nearing the towers of Asgard. The gods were waiting anxiously. They knew who the falcon was and what it was carrying. They saw the eagle bearing down on the falcon and knew that everything depended on rescuing Loki's precious burden. Hurriedly they threw together a great heap of wood chips and kindling and, just as the eagle approached the walls, they lit the pile. The eagle was flying much too fast to stop. It flew into the flames, its feathers caught fire, the wings shriveled, and the monstrous bird-giant burned to death.

Shouts of joy rang through Asgard. Everyone embraced. Loki was forgiven because of his daring rescue. Iduna was with them again, the apples were safe, and the gods once more were young.

SIEGFRIED

...Who Knew No Fear

IEGFRIED's father, a hero of the Walsung clan, had been killed in combat and his mother had fled to a cave belonging to the dwarf Mime, a misshapen smith and one of the Nibelung tribe. There she had died after giving birth to a boy, and there Siegfried had been brought up by Mime to be a strong youth, at home in the forest, in tune with everything wild, and afraid of nothing. Mime had reared the boy with a purpose, not for love but for greed.

Fafner, a giant who had transformed himself into a dragon, occupied another cave in the forest; he guarded the Rhinegold, the fabulous treasure hoard complete with a magic helmet, the Tarnhelm, which made its wearer invisible, and the Ring which made its owner all powerful. It was this gold and this power which Mime wanted. He knew he could never face the dragon but, equipped with the right kind of sword, Siegfried could overcome the monster and bring the treasure back to Mime.

The Nibelung dwarf toiled at his forge, attempting to make the needed sword. Desperately he sent up the flames, worked the bellows, and struck the anvil. Hammering away at a new sword-blade, he muttered bitterly.

"Useless effort! Every sword I make, Siegfried breaks in two as if it were rotten wood. He smashes the toughest steel across his knee and laughs like a child breaking a toy. There is only one sword that is invulnerable—his father's sword. It was the gift of a god, and it was broken by a god. Siegfried's mother carried the pieces with her and gave them to me for her son. 'Some day he will need it,' she said. 'Put the pieces together for him.' Easier said than done! How many

times I have tried to weld those pieces into one! There is a magic—
or a curse—about them that will not let them be reforged. So here
I try once more, and once more it will be useless."

A joyful shout. Mime dropped his hammer, and young Siegfried
burst into the cave. He led a bear by a rope as casually as though
he were bringing in a dog. Mime shrieked, Siegfried laughed, and,
with a pat on the rump, sent the bear back to the forest. He picked
up the sword which Mime had just made and snapped it with the
twist of his wrist.

"You call yourself a craftsman!" Siegfried cried. "You're a blunderer
and a coward! And stupid! The animals are much better company.
I wonder why I ever come back here."

"You come back because I'm like a father to you. I teach you
things. I give you food. Look—here is a stew I've saved for your
supper."

"Take it away. It gives me a stomachache just to smell it. And it
gives me a headache just to look at you."

"That's the reward I get for all my pains," whined Mime. "I serve
you not only as a father but as a mother. I spend my life doing
things for you. I work and worry. I clothe you and cook for you. No
mother could do more."

Siegfried interrupted him. "Tell me about my mother. And my
father, too. What were their names? Where did they come from?
Tell me! If you don't, I'll choke the words or the life out of you!"

"Take your hands away from my throat," gasped Mime. "There's
little to tell. I can't give you names. All I know is that a woman
dragged herself to this cave some years ago. She was ill—her husband had been mysteriously killed—she showed me the broken
pieces of his sword. Just before she died, she bore a boy child and
told me to call him Siegfried. She blessed me for taking care of you
and—"

"That's enough," said Siegfried. "Where are the pieces of my
father's sword? Why have you hidden them from me?"

"They are useless," said Mime.

"Useless?" mocked Siegfried. "They were made to use. And use
them I will. See that the parts are put together. Forge them for me at
once." And off he dashed to the forest.

With his head in his hands Mime sat in despair. He looked up as
a shadow fell across the floor of the cave. He was faced by a tall
stranger muffled in a dark blue cloak and a hat that came down over
one eye.

"Who are you?" asked Mime.

"They call me Wanderer," replied the stranger, "for I wander up and down the earth. I have come here because I am told you are a wise and clever man. I myself am not altogether without some knowledge. Let us have a game. You will ask me three questions; then I will ask you three. Whoever loses will lose his head. Agreed?"

Mime considered himself anyone's equal when it came to intelligence. Without hesitation he said, "Agreed."

"First," he asked, "who dwell in the dark caverns and depths of the earth?"

"The Nibelungs," replied Wanderer.

"Second," said Mime, "who live on the surface of earth?"

"The giants," answered Wanderer.

"Third," said Mime, "who inhabit the cloudy heights and the sky?"

"The gods," said Wanderer and rose to his feet. As he uttered the words he struck the ground with his staff and there was a low peal of thunder. Mime trembled, for he suspected that Wanderer was none other than the one-eyed Wotan, sometimes called Odin, the supreme god. Trembling and fearful, Mime braced himself for the questions he must answer or forfeit his head.

"It is my turn now," said Wanderer. "Who, among men, are those whom Wotan loves most and yet treats so badly?"

"I know that well," replied Mime confidently. "A tribe called the Walsungs, especially Siegmund and Sieglinde, and their son Siegfried."

"And how is Siegfried going to overcome the dragon who guards the precious Rhinegold?"

"I know the answer to that, too," replied Mime promptly. "With his father's invincible sword."

"You have answered two questions rightly," said Wanderer. "Now tell me who is going to put that sword together again?"

Mime cowered. He looked like a trapped animal. "I do not know," he groaned.

"Then I will tell you," said the god. "It will be put together by one who does not know the meaning of fear. As for your head, I won't claim it as a forfeit. Keep it a little while, for you will lose it to the one who has never known what fear is."

The Wanderer strode from the cave, and another rumble of thunder echoed his scornful laugh. As he left, Siegfried returned.

"Well," said Siegfried, "where is my sword. Haven't you put the pieces together yet?"

"The invincible sword?" Mime whimpered. "I cannot mend it. It can be fashioned only by one who does not know the meaning of fear."

"Fear?" said Siegfried. "What is fear?"

"It is what you feel when you are alone in the deep forest," whispered Mime. "When night falls suddenly and the cold creeps out of the earth and the trees stretch out ghostly branches and your breath comes fast with fear."

"If that is fear," said Siegfried, "I've never felt it. What else?"

"Have you never lost your way in the woods, heard the animals growling and feared that they would attack you?"

"Why would they attack me? The animals are my friends."

"You are a boastful boy," said Mime. "You would not be so brave if you had to face the dragon whose cave is at the other end of the forest. His breath scorches everything within fifty feet of him; fire comes out of his nostrils; his venom burns the flesh off his victims; he strangles and devours any man who approaches him. The dragon will teach you fear."

"You do not make me afraid," said Siegfried. "You only make me curious. Lead me to the dragon so I may feel what fear is like. First I must have the sword. Here! Give me the pieces!"

Mime handed them to him. "What are you going to do with them?"

"You will see," said Siegfried, and began to reduce the metal to filings. Then he melted them and set to work to forge the sword. As the flames leaped in the air, Siegfried sang. "A sword is needed, and a sword I will have! Here, in a baptism of fire, I will name the sword. It will be called Needful. Needful it is and Needful it will be!"

He hammered, shaped, and sharpened the steel. Finally the marvelous weapon emerged. He tested its strength and toughness. Raising it over his head, he crashed it down on the iron anvil. The anvil broke in two.

"Now," cried Siegfried, "I am ready for your dragon!"

Mime, according to his plan, guided Siegfried to the dragon's cave.

"This is the place," said Mime. "The dragon is sleeping inside. When you rouse him, look out for his jaws; they can snap a man's bones as easily as you snap twigs. Don't stand in front of him. Remember his breath is poison."

"I will wait until he comes out to drink," said Siegfried. "Until then I want to be alone. Go away."

Mime left, and Siegfried stretched himself out under the trees.

The air was still. A soft breeze murmured through the leaves. It caressed him gently, like a soothing hand, and he thought of the mother he never knew. The beauty of the forest flowed over him; everything quivered with warmth and wonder. A bird trilled a liquid melody and Siegfried tried to imitate it. He made holes in a reed and blew through it. But the notes were nothing like the bird's, and he tossed the poor instrument aside.

"I'll make my own music," cried Siegfried. He sounded a blast on his horn—and the dragon awoke. Roaring, he came out of the cave, belching fire and smoke.

"Is that the way to teach me fear?" laughed Siegfried. "I can make a better fire with dried grass."

Angered by the youth's brashness, the dragon struck at him, but Siegfried sprang to one side and wounded the monster in the tail. The dragon bellowed in wrath and, as he rose to crush his assailant, Siegfried plunged Needful into its heart. Fatally wounded, the dragon who was once a giant closed its burning eyes. It spoke.

"You have youth and courage," breathed the dragon heavily. "But you do not know what you have done. You have done this thing for someone else. Beware of him who brought you here. It is he who will profit by this murder. Beware." With these words the dragon died.

Siegfried reached out a hand in pity, and a drop of the dragon's blood fell on it. It was magic blood—and suddenly Siegfried understood what the bird's song meant. The bird told him what Mime had never told him: that there was a treasure in the cave, and that it comprised not only a vast amount of gold but also the Tarnhelm, which can make its wearer invisible, and the Ring of the Nibelungs which can give its owner power over the world. When Siegfried emerged from the cave, carrying the Tarnhelm and wearing the Ring, the bird sang again.

"Siegfried, listen carefully," the bird said. "Fafner the dragon was right. Mime plots to do away with you. When he has killed you, he plans to take the Rhinegold, the Tarnhelm, and the Ring which will make him ruler of the world. First he will try to persuade you do do what he wants. He will flatter you; he will use honeyed words. But the power of the dragon's blood will let you understand what he means, not what he says. You will be able to read his mind."

As the bird predicted, when they met, Mime complimented Siegfried on his brave deed. He tried to coax Siegfried into trusting him. But Siegfried did not listen to the words. Instead, he heard Mime's thoughts. He learned that Mime really hated him, that he had brought him up only to get the treasure, and that he intended to kill Siegfried with Siegfried's own sword.

"You are tired," said Mime, pretending he was concerned about Siegfried. "I've brought you a cooling potion. Drink. It will refresh you."

But Siegfried knew that the potion was poisoned, that it would not refresh him but put him to sleep, a sleep from which he would never wake. He wasted no words on Mime, but struck him down with one blow of his sword and threw the body into the cave.

"Here is what you wanted," he said contemptuously. "I will take only the Tarnhelm and the Ring. Keep the rest of the precious treasure. Guard it well."

Sick at heart and weary, he lay down again. Loneliness overcame him.

"Will I never know true companionship? Will I never feel the affection of another human being?"

Again the bird sang. "Far away on a rocky mountaintop," sang the bird, "there lies the loveliest of creatures, a true goddess. She is asleep, surrounded by a ring of fire. She will not open her eyes until someone brave enough to go through that fire awakens her. You who know no fear, shall I lead you to Brunnhilde?"

"Lead!" cried Siegfried delightedly. "I will follow. To the mountaintop through flood and fire! I come!"

It was a long journey, but Siegfried was tireless. He reached the mountain, but there was still a long climb to the top. The night was black, the wind was wild, the way was blocked by boulders. Standing among the rocks was a shrouded figure. It was Wanderer, the god Wotan, who had protected his daughter, Brunnhilde, with the ring of fire. He waited to find out if the one who sought her was worthy of her. At dawn he saw Siegfried making his way among the rocks. Wotan stopped him.

"This is no place for mortals," he said. "Return or fear my wrath."

"I fear no one's wrath," said Siegfried. "I have slain a fire-breathing dragon. I have drunk dragon's blood. I shall go up this mountain to face more fire, and I shall hardly be stopped by a foolish old man."

"You are a reckless youth," said Wotan. "You do not know to whom you speak. You must answer me. Tell me first who forged the sword you carry?"

"I did," said Siegfried curtly. "There's been enough talk. Out of my way!"

"Foolish boy. This will stop you." With a lordly gesture Wotan interposed his spear, but Siegfried shattered it with his sword, Needful. There was a flash of lightning and Wotan picked up the pieces of his broken power.

"Go onward," he told Siegfried, half in sorrow, half in admiration. "You cannot be stopped."

Over the rocks and through the fire Siegfried passed. Unharmed he reached the rock on which Brunnhilde lay sleeping under a sky of the most brilliant blue. She was clad in shining armor, the visor of her helmet was down, and Siegfried assumed the figure was a man.

"The bird misled me," he said. "This is a warrior, not a woman. I shall wake him with a challenge."

He removed the helmet, and a cascade of golden hair spilled out. Siegfried was astonished. He cut the ties which held the armor together, and saw a soft body clad in white. Bewildered, wondering if what he felt was fear, he bent over the beautiful form and instinctively pressed his lips to hers.

Brunnhilde opened her eyes. Slowly she raised herself and lifted her arms to the sun. "Hail, blessed light," she cried. "Hail, O Sun, from whose beams I have been banished so long a time. And hail, blessed hero, who went through the fire to come to me. Know that I was once a goddess, Wotan's daughter, one of the Valkyries. Now I give up my divinity for mortality and the love of a mortal. The daughter of a god has become a woman, a woman who shall live for her rescuer, her treasure of treasures, her all-in-all."

Siegfried echoed her rapture. "Together we shall live laughing. Laughing with love, laughing at death," he cried, and took her in his arms.

BEOWULF

... *The Fight with Grendel*

EOWULF is a savage tale written a thousand years ago by an Anglo-Saxon poet. The scene is laid in Denmark, but the story, which runs to more than three thousand lines, is told in Old English. The story is full of violence made beautiful by the way the language was used. The original lines were strangely musical because so many of the words began with the same sound. They were also vivid with "kennings," words that were in themselves pictures of what they described. The sun was "the sky-candle," the sea was "the whale's road," a ship was "a sea-horse," a battle was "spear-play," a wife was "the weaver of peace," a ruler was "the ring-giver," the room in which the warriors drank mead (a mixture of honey, malt, and water) was "the mead-hall," and Beowulf himself was a "bee-wolf," a nickname for a bear.

The story began in the mead-hall of Hrothgar, king of the Danes. It was a high hall with many pinnacles, and in it there was much rejoicing. There were songs celebrating Hrothgar's victories and, when the warriors lifted their cups of mead, they were charmed by the sound of the harp, called "glee-wood" because its music was good and gleeful to hear. The harpist, or "glee-man," sang how the Almighty made the fair earth and the waters surrounding it, how he set the sun and moon in the sky to light the world, how he adorned every part of the land with foliage, flower, and fruit, how he sent life into everything that breathes and moves.

Night came and the warriors slept. They did not sleep long. A hideous monster, Grendel, broke into the hall and slew thirty heroes. This was only the beginning. For twelve years Grendel, fierce and furious, ravaged the country. Hrothgar and his men were powerless to oppose the gigantic beast. Night after night it crept through the misty moors and, in the dark shadow of death, trapped young and old. Many mighty men sat in council, debating what could be done to stop the terror of Grendel. They planned, they prayed, they offered sacrifices, but nothing availed.

Far away, in the distant country of the Geats, a young hero, Beowulf, heard of the havoc caused by Grendel. He did not hesitate. With fourteen other warriors, Beowulf set sail over the whale's road. Coming to help Hrothgar, the gallant fifteen were welcomed with a great feast. When they stood up in their coats of mail and clashing battle-raiment, the cheers were loud and long. Hrothgar had grown old, but he exulted in the hope that the young hero would succeed where all others had failed.

"I knew him when he was a child," said Hrothgar. "Now he has come as a loyal friend. I have heard that he is brave in battle, that the grip of his hand holds the swiftest of swords, and that he has the strength and thrust of thirty men. Happy am I to hail him."

"Hail!" echoed everyone. "Hail!"

"Happy am I to be here," said Beowulf. "It will not be my first fight with the forces of evil. I have disposed of enemies, destroyed giants, and slain the fearful sea-beasts that ride the surf. I ask one thing only. Let me take on the task of getting rid of Grendel by myself. I have learned that the monster is proof against weapons. Therefore I scorn to carry a sword to strike or even a shield to shelter me. I will grapple with the fiend and fight it, life for life, foe against foe. You will not have to bury me if I fail. The beast will bear my body away. But I do not fear the outcome. I will fight, and Fate will decide."

"Glad am I that you came," said Hrothgar. "Yet am I ashamed to have to hope for help. But the best of my men are gone, my warrior-band has melted away. How many times the warriors have sat, sword in hand, awaiting the onset of Grendel. And how many times I have found the benches stained with blood, the hall littered with the dead. But enough of this. Sit now to the feast, and let us talk of nothing but victory."

After the feasting, the toasting and boasting, Beowulf and his group were left alone. He lay down, but he did not sleep. Wakeful, he waited for the dread destroyer, the ruthless ranger who was stalking through the gloom of the night.

Grendel drew near. This was not the first time that he had

haunted Hrothgar's home. He knew every corner and cranny of the room. Hoping to pounce on his prey, he roared into the hall. His eyes flamed; his mouth gaped; his tongue slavered. He licked his lips expecting a plentiful feast. He saw Beowulf.

This was the moment. As the fiend started to clutch Beowulf with his frightful claw, Beowulf quickly grasped it and fastened on the arm. Grendel was caught off guard. He attempted to pull loose, to flee and rejoin the horde of demons of which he was the worst. But Beowulf held on. They threshed about like maddened wrestlers. Benches were uprooted, tables thrown about, the hall shook, the walls trembled, the whole building itself seemed ready to crash. Both opponents staggered and then, with his bare hands, Beowulf tore Grendel's arm clear out of its socket. With a hideous howl, the monster rushed to the fen where it lived and where it was to die. As a token of the fight, Beowulf hung his trophy on the wall: the claw and arm of Grendel which would never harm anyone again.

The limb did not hang there long. At midnight Grendel's mother came to avenge her son. She slew the guard and stole the severed arm. Beowulf pursued her and plunged into the filthy pond that was her home. Demons fought with him; their slimy arms tried to bury him in the mud. But he fought them off and attacked Grendel's mother. The struggle was long, but finally Beowulf got a strangle-hold and, with a desperate stroke, cut off her head.

Thus triumphed Beowulf, brave and bold warrior, "kindest of kinsmen and keenest for fame."

RAMA

...The Bow That Could Not Be Bent

AMA is the hero of the *Ramayana,* a major epic of India written about 300 B.C. Like many ancient works, such as the Greek *Odyssey* and the Anglo-Saxon *Beowulf,* the *Ramayana* is full of legends that tell of impossible tasks, dangerous hazards, and wonderful victories.

Rama had been brought up in the court of his father, King Dasaratha. By the time he was sixteen he was more mature than most men. His body had been hardened by countless exercises and preparations for manhood. He was expert in wrestling, running, horsemanship, and swordsmanship. His mind had been developed by studies in philosophy, mathematics, and music. He was ready for whatever life had to offer.

One day an elderly sage entered the court and was given an audience.

"I was once a king," said the sage. "But I gave up the throne for a better way of life. It is for the less worldly life that I make a request."

"As one who is still worldly, I listen," said Dasaratha. "Name your request, and I will try to grant it."

"Let me have your son, Rama, for a while," said the sage. "He seems prepared for any adventure. He is strong in body and sound in mind. But he knows little of the spirit. Let me show him the potency of meditation and the power of prayer."

Dasaratha hesitated. "You ask me to give you the joy of my middle years and the hope of my old age. It is asking a great deal."

"I ask it not only for Rama's sake but also for the sake of the people," said the sage. "Our village has been ruined by a super-natural monster. It is spreading terror through the rest of the country. Only one who combines physical prowess with spiritual strength can defeat it. That is why I ask for Rama."

Before Dasaratha could reply, Rama spoke up. "Father, let me go. I would gladly learn what I lack. Even more gladly would I rid the country of the monster. I beseech you, let me go."

"I cannot deny you your right to learn," said Dasaratha. "And I would not hinder you from employing all your powers, especially in a good cause. So be it. You may go."

The way to the sage's village was long. It took months of travel. On the journey Rama was instructed in prayers, chants, and meditations.

"Your soul is now as pure as your body is perfect," said the sage. "You are religion itself. Now you are ready for whatever may befall."

As though to challenge those words, the air thundered with an earth-shaking roar. A huge elephant-like creature with wicked tusks like ten-foot-long spears and a head like a burning furnace charged upon them. Rama sped arrow after arrow at the monster but, though he wounded it, the monster continued to thrust at them with its death-dealing tusks. Rama uttered a prayer for survival and shot his last arrow. It tore through the air, a fearful shaft of lightning, and lodged in the monster's throat. Black smoke curled from its mouth like a horde of writhing serpents, and its death-cry shattered the trees.

"Evil cannot touch you," said the sage. "Now let us see if your strength of purpose is great enough to bend the bow that has never been bent."

"What bow is that?" inquired Rama.

"In Mithila lives the loveliest, most flowerlike beauty ever born. She is Sita, daughter of King Janaka. Ever since her fifteenth year, princes have come from all over India to woo her. Her father has forbidden anyone to court her who cannot pass one particular test. He must bend the bow—the bow of everlasting power—the bow which cannot be bent."

"I would like to see that bow," said Rama. "And I would also like to look upon the lovely Sita. Let us go to Mithila."

After four days' journeying, they reached the capital at night. It was a superb city, blazing with lights of every conceivable color. Royal banners snapped in the air, bursts of music greeted the visitors. They could not wait for what morning would bring.

A king's son, Rama was used to luxury. But when he stood before King Janaka in the high vaulted throne-room walled in marble set with rubies, sapphires, and emeralds, he knew that he had never seen anything as magnificent. Then, looking at Sita who sat next to her father, he knew he had never seen anything as desirable. She returned his gaze and smiled. He had never seen her before, yet he seemed to recognize her. Perhaps she was some divinity he had worshiped in a dream. Perhaps he had known her in some other life. Perhaps, in that other life, he had been her lover. But it was this life that Rama was now thinking about. He drew in his breath sharply as a herald announced that the ceremonies were about to begin.

First there was music: flute-playing punctuated by the light clashing of finger-cymbals, the low-droning tamboura, and singing accompanied by the sitar, a magically stringed instrument named in honor of the princess. Then there was solemn dancing, the performers weaving to and fro like plumed birds following some slow and half-forgotten ritual. Then there was the hour of meditation. Then six servants brought in the bow.

"As you see," said King Janaka, "it takes six men to carry the bow. It is difficult enough to lift and it has never been bent. There is a prophecy that it can be lifted only by the bravest and that only the purest as well as the strongest can bend it. Does anyone care to attempt the trial?"

The bow was placed upon velvet cushions and a young noble with jewels in his turban came forward. He took hold of the bow, but try as he might, it would not be budged. A second youth, a tall prince from Hindustan, grasped the bow, strained to raise it an inch, and fell on his face. A third, a fourth, and a fifth failed equally. All the contestants drew back in shame, their eyes fixed on the bow as if it were a deadly python.

Sita had shown no interest in the proceedings. Now she looked at Rama. He moved toward the velvet cushions, bowed to the king, and bowed even more deeply to Sita. He clasped his hands, bent his head, and uttered a silent prayer. Then he put his hands on the bow

and slowly lifted it to his ankles, then his knees, then his chest, and then, still slowly but without exerting himself, Rama lifted it above his head. The murmur that ran through the room was a mixture of admiration and astonishment. The murmur grew to shouts as Rama took the two ends of the bow in his hands and bent it until the two ends touched. Then, placing the bow across his knee, he snapped it in half as though it were a slender staff. The shouting threatened to crack the marble walls.

Then there was silence as the king left his throne to place a crown on Rama's head. And when Rama looked at Sita, it was she who bowed. It was the bow of a loving wife waiting to serve her lord.

GULAM

...The Jar of Rice

ESOP has a fable about a milkmaid and a pail of milk, a fable that shows we cannot get what we want merely by wishing for it or dreaming about it. In India there is a similar tale with a similar ending. It concerns a lazy countryman by the name of Gulam who managed to beg some rice from his more industrious neighbors. He put the grains of rice in a clay jar and set it on a table.

"Now," said Gulam, sitting down, "that's all I need to make me rich. Soon I will drop these grains of rice in the damp earth. Then the rains will come, the water will cover the land, the grains will take root, the seedlings will come up, and I will have a great crop of rice. But I won't sell it right away. I'll wait for a famine—there are always famines in India—and then I'll sell my rice for a large amount of money. With the money I will buy a herd of Brahman cattle. There will be many calves, and these I will sell to farmers throughout the country. With the profit from the sales I will put up stables for the finest breed of horses in India. Keeping the brood mares, I will sell the colts for polo ponies and the stallions to the cavalry. Soon I will be the owner of a large estate.

"By that time I will be ready to get married, but I will take my time selecting a bride. I will ignore my neighbors and wait until rich men come to me offering their daughters. I will choose the one that is the most beautiful and brings the largest dowry. I will have six sons. I will build a huge house for myself and my wife, and separate houses for each of my growing sons. There will be a dozen

153

barns not only for horses and cattle but for water buffaloes, and there will be palisades for elephants.

"Then," said Gulam, rising to his feet, "then I will invite the neighbors over. 'See,' I will say, 'what the man you thought lazy has accomplished. Look at those grand houses on the left! See those big barns on the right! Watch as the horses and water buffaloes and even the elephants obey me when I wave my hands!' "

Striding around the rooms, he waved his hands—and hit the clay jar. It fell to the floor and broke. The rice spilled and, before the man could scoop it up, was blown away by the wind. Now he had nothing—no cattle, no horses, no elephants, no houses, no barns, no wife, no children—not even a grain of rice.

The moral in this story is the same as in Aesop's fable. Don't count your chickens before they are hatched.

SOHRAB AND RUSTUM

...The Tragic Encounter

THE MEETING of a father and a son who did not know each other was a theme well known to the ancient story-tellers. It lost none of its dramatic power when retold in "Sohrab and Rustum" by the English poet Matthew Arnold in the nineteenth century.

Rustum, mightiest of Persia's warriors, had ridden with his retinue into Ader-baijan and had been entertained with great feasts by the king of the country. There he had fallen in love with the king's daughter, married her, and remained awhile at the king's court, hoping his wife would bear him a son. An outbreak of war called him back to Persia, and when his son was born, the mother feared his father would take him away to fight and probably be killed. She sent a messenger to Rustum telling him that the child was a girl. Rustum was too occupied to make further inquiries and continued his career as champion of Persia.

The boy, Sohrab, grew up tall and heavy-muscled, in all respects like his father. He had heard countless tales of Rustum's heroic deeds and longed to meet him. His mother did all she could to dissuade him from a military life, but when he was eighteen he ran away to find his father. Hoping to win Rustum's regard on his own merits, Sohrab decided not to go to Persia and ask favors. Instead he joined the Tartar army, where he soon obtained wide renown.

Sohrab became famous for his swordmanship and his daring. His reputation as a warrior grew greater than anyone's except Rustum's. The Tartars were so proud of him that they declared no one in the world could be found willing to stand up to Sohrab in single combat. This irritated the Persians. "We must throw this boast back into their teeth," they muttered. They came to Rustum. "You must put a stop to their bluster. Only you can save us from shame."

Rustum had had enough of warfare. "I am content never to draw a sword again," he said. "I would be glad to have had such a son as Sohrab, but that has been denied me. The battlefield belongs to the young. Let them have it."

The Persians would not accept Rustum's withdrawal. "What will men say?" they argued. "Must we tell people that when Sohrab, a youth of unknown origin, defied us, our bravest warrior hid his face? Shall we tell them that the great Rustum is afraid of a younger man?"

Rustum was provoked. "You know better. You know I fear no one. Very well. But, if I must give up peace and quiet, I will fight as an unknown with plain arms."

He strode to his tent and let his servants equip him with ordinary armor. When they brought his battle shield, he waved it away. "It bears my emblem, the lion-headed griffin," he said. "It is a device that will be recognized, and I will not take advantage of my reputation."

When he approached the place chosen for the combat, Sohrab came from the Tartar tent. Rustum could not help but admire him. The sight of the tall adventurous youth also moved him to pity.

"Give up this contest," he said mildly. "I am an old, experienced warrior. You are young. I have never lost a fight or failed to slay my foe. You have a life to live."

Sohrab stiffened, but he said nothing.

"If you must fight," said Rustum, "fight on my side. Fight under my banner as though you were my son."

Sohrab looked at Rustum's figure standing like a mighty tower, and he had an intuition. "Can you be Rustum?" he asked. "Tell me, are you not he?"

Rustum was suspicious. If I tell this young man who I am, he thought to himself, he will find some excuse not to fight, but flatter me and shake my hand. Later, he will boast that he and I met as equals and, being so much younger, he generously spared my life. Out loud he said, "What is this about Rustum? If Rustum were here you would know it. Men look at Rustum and run. I am here to answer your challenge. Will you withdraw it? Or will you fight?"

"You may be older and more tried, but you are not readier than I," said Sohrab. "Begin!"

Both men threw their spears. They struck against the shields, but neither combatant was hurt. Then Rustum seized a heavy club and struck at Sohrab. The youth sprang nimbly aside, and the weight of the club made Rustum lose his balance. He fell, and Sohrab could have killed him with his sword. Instead, Sohrab drew back.

"It was a good blow," he said, "but it was too hard. I do not know who you are, but you have touched something in me. Let us plant our spears in the sand and declare a truce."

Rustum would not hear of it. Quivering with rage and shame, he shouted. "You are quick on your feet. But this is not a dance. Any pity I had for you is gone. Draw your sword!"

The two men rushed together. Their shields clanged, their swords clashed, their helmets were dented, their armor was torn. The elements seemed to take part in the conflict, for a storm sprang up, whipping sand into their eyes. Half blinded, they fought on until their swords were hacked into saws. Thunder roared, and as the lightning flashed, Rustum shouted his battle cry, "Rustum!"

Hearing the name, Sohrab was bewildered. He paused a moment, looking around him. The pause was fatal. In that moment Rustum's spear pierced his side and Sohrab sank wounded on the bloody soil.

"The name was my undoing," said Sohrab. "But it is he, Rustum, my father, who will avenge my death."

"What talk is this of fathers and revenge?" said Rustum. "Rustum never had a son."

"He had indeed," said Sohrab, his voice weakening, "and that lost son am I. Some day Rustum will learn the truth. He will be saddened, but not so much as my mother."

"Who is your mother?" said Rustum anxiously.

"A king's daughter," whispered Sohrab. "In Ader-baijan."

"But she—she bore only one child—a girl," stammered Rustum. "Someone must have misinformed you. Or you are lying."

"Dying men do not lie," said Sohrab faintly. "Here is proof—here on my arm."

Rustum looked and saw, tattooed on Sohrab's arm, his own emblem, the lion-headed griffin. Speechless, he smote his head and sank to earth. Then he uttered a single, agonized cry, "My son!" Crawling to where Sohrab lay, he cast his arms about the boy's neck and kissed his lips. Stroking the pale cheeks, he tried to call Sohrab back to life, but in vain. The only life that remained was Rustum's—a life he no longer wanted.

ILMARINEN

...*How He Won His Bride*

T HE *Kalevala* is the Finnish national epic composed three thousand years ago and containing more than twenty thousand verses. It has a wide sweeping story and a rich, rolling sound—Longfellow borrowed the meter for *The Song of Hiawatha*.

The long poem begins with a mythical account of the origin of the world, but it centers about the three sons of Kaleva: Lemminkainen, the gigantic cavalier; Vainamoinen, the musician; and Ilmarinen, the wonder-smith.

It was Ilmarinen, the youngest, who made the Sampo, a magical mill which, according to desire, produced salt, food, and gold, and brought fortune to its owner. And it was Ilmarinen who set out to win the fabulous daughter of Louhi, a chief of Pohjola in the eternally frozen north. Vainamoinen had hoped that Louhi's daughter might be his bride, but he soon realized he could not compete with his cleverer brother.

Before he started north, Ilmarinen did everything he could to dazzle and delight any girl. He prepared a sauna bath, gathered stones and heated them until they gave off a white steam, sweated over them until his body shone, then beat himself lightly with birch boughs so that his skin was a glowing pink. He put on a white linen shirt, white stockings, and new white trousers. Over this he wore a coat of the whitest wool and covered his head and ears with a heavy cap of white fox fur. He polished the iron sleigh that he had forged, threw a white bearskin on the seat, and decorated the dashboard with six golden birds he had fashioned. He harnessed two white horses, cracked his whip, and shouted, "Off we go!"

It was weeks before he reached Pohjola. His blood had almost turned to ice, but the cold was dispelled by Louhi's warm welcome.

"Stay in Pohjola as long as you wish," said Louhi. "But I am afraid you will not stay long. I know what you have come for and what you would like to carry away. I should warn you it will not be easy. I have kept my daughter hidden from men. There are three things you must do before you can have her. If you can do the first thing, I will let you look at her. If you can accomplish the second, you may touch her hand and, perhaps, win her smile. But only after you have accomplished the third will you be allowed to take her with you—that is, if she is willing."

"It is proper that you should set three tasks," said Ilmarinen. "And it is proper that I should try to perform them. What is the first thing I must do?"

"You must plow a field which is full of serpents," said Louhi. "And you must plow every inch of it without killing a single snake."

Ilmarinen had brought his forge with him. He now proceeded to construct a plow of silver with an edge so sharp that when it cut through the earth it produced a wild hissing sound. As soon as Ilmarinen made the first furrow, the snakes heard the loud hiss and thought they were being pursued by some sort of huge viper. They slithered away and left the field clear for Ilmarinen. He then cultivated the field to the last inch.

"Now you may look at my daughter," said Louhi. "Is she not fair?"

Fair she was, but cold and silent. She stood as though she were carved in ice. Ilmarinen was not dismayed.

"She is a true daughter of the Northland," said Ilmarinen. "I would like to touch her and see if there is flesh and blood beneath that frozen surface."

"That you can do if you perform the second task," said Louhi. "It is to go to the dark forest, find the wolf that kills but is never seen, and bring it back alive."

Again Ilmarinen went to his forge. This time he mad a muzzle of flexible metal and a chain of silver links. Then he went to the dark woods and waited until nightfall. When the moon rose. Ilmarinen barked, barked like a dog baying at the moon. The barking was answered by a blood-curdling howl, and a black wolf sprang out of the forest. It was easy to slip the muzzle over the wolf's jaw and lead it, cowed, back to Pohjola.

Once more Louhi's daughter stood before Ilmarinen. This time

he touched her hand and found it warm. Warmer still was the smile she gave him.

"The third task is the hardest," said Louhi. "It is to catch the pike that lives among the rocks and rapids of the arctic river. It is, I should warn you, a gigantic fish and it has scales that are made of steel. Its teeth are daggers; they can bite through bone. What's more, it is so strong and swift that no net can hold it. Get that pike for me."

Ilmarinen went to his forge for the third time. He made a bird out of pure bronze, a bird so huge that, compared to it, an eagle seemed as small as a sparrow. Its beak was like a sword and its claws were razor-edged knives. When he attached the wings, he put something in the bronze bird so it could fly. Then he got on its back and directed it toward the arctic river.

The giant pike was sunning itself on the surface when it saw the huge bronze bird circling above the stream. The fish dived among the rocks. But the bronze bird was faster. It swooped through the air, plunged into the river, and fastened its razor-edged claws into the pike's eyes. Blinded, the fish threshed about, trying to drag its attacker under the water. But the bird held fast, stabbing and striking until it thrust its sword-like beak into the pike's heart. There was a terrible shudder, and the pike lay still. Then the bronze bird soared into the air and Ilmarinen brought the huge fish home.

"No fish will ever taste as sweet as this one when it is cooked," said Louhi. "But you will not stay for the banquet?"

"I have something else in mind," said Ilmarinen.

"I think I can guess what it is," said Louhi. "I will tell you the truth, Ilmarinen. Because you are a clever man and a wonder-smith, you passed all three tests. But even if you had failed every one, my daughter would still have been yours. After your first test, she pretended not to notice you. But before that, the moment she saw you, she had made up her mind. She knew she would go with you if you would take her."

Louhi clapped his hands and the girl entered the room. She looked straight at Ilmarinen and, without a word, walked into his arms.

LEIF THE LUCKY

...What He Discovered

HE VIKINGS were great seafarers and great fighters—the name Viking means "sea-warrior"—and they came from Scandinavia. Beginning in the eighth century, for hundreds of years they roamed and raided. They lived for adventure, which was another name for plunder. Pillaging country after country, they invaded Europe, England, Scotland, and Ireland.

The Viking ships were something like the Roman galleys, but the so-called "long boats" were built for rougher weather than their Roman models. They had wide and heavy sails, but in battle as well as voyaging, they depended on the number and strength of the rowers. The largest were said to have had twenty benches on each side, forty oars, and they rowed in shifts, relays of sixty to eighty men, day and night. Their bulwarks were hung with the warriors' shields, and the prows were carved to resemble the heads of weird creatures, usually dragons.

In the tenth century Eric the Red lived in Iceland. Like his father, who had been forced to leave Norway, Eric the Red was a violent man. He was so wild that the people turned against him and he became an outlaw. He ravaged the Scandinavian seacoast, and went on to sail for strange countries. Sailing to the west, he discovered Greenland and founded a colony there.

Leif Ericsson, son of Eric the Red, inherited his father's prowess as seaman and passion for discovery. But his was a much milder nature than most of the clan's. At this time Christianity was beginning to replace the worship of the Norse gods. Odin and Thor were still feared, but a more merciful religion was taking hold. When Leif visited the court of Olaf Tryggvason in Norway, his gentle manner made such an impression that the king urged him to return to Greenland and preach Christianity there.

As soon as he had embarked with his crew, Leif ran into bad weather. Contrary winds drove him far off his course; storm after storm threatened to wreck his ship; the tiller was often wrenched out of the steersman's hand.

At last land was sighted. It was a new land, a land of which they had no knowledge whatever. Going ashore, Leif was delighted with all he saw. The country was rich with green things growing everywhere. There was abundant wheat and corn and, spreading over the hills, there were luxurious vines heavy with wild grapes. He called the place Vinland.

That was in the year 1000. Leif did not know that he had found a new continent. Almost five hundred years before Columbus crossed the Atlantic, Leif the Lucky had discovered America.

KING ARTHUR

...*The Shield and the Hammer*

NE SPRING morning in the sixth century, while riding through the countryside, King Arthur of Britain and his court came upon a lamentable sight. A young squire led a horse that carried a knight bleeding badly from a gash in his side. As soon as they stopped, the knight fell to the ground. The king gave orders to bring the knight to the castle where his wounds could be treated, but it was obvious that the man was dying. King Arthur turned to the squire.

"What happened?" he asked.

"My master, Sir Miles, and I were riding through the woods when, at the end of the day, we saw a castle a little way beyond a bridge. We were about to seek hospitality when we noticed a huge tree on which a large number of shields were hung. That seemed strange. Stranger still was something at the entrance to the bridge. A black shield was attached to a post. Beside it was a brass hammer. Underneath there was a sign that read: 'Whoever smites this shield with this hammer must be willing to risk his life.' It was a challenge that no true knight could ignore. My master did not hesitate for a moment. He seized the hammer, struck the shield, and before the echoes stopped ringing, a black knight charged across the bridge. My master barely had time to prepare for the assault. As he leveled his lance the black knight drove his spear through my master's shield and into his side. Then he took the shield and hung it upon the tree with all the others. Though my master was mortally hurt, he did not cry out while I got him on his horse and brought him here."

"This must be avenged," said King Arthur. "Which one of my court will challenge that knight whose heart is as black as his armor, who not only leaves a fallen knight to bleed on the ground but also takes away his shield?"

All sprang forward, but Griflet was the first to speak.

"Let me earn my spurs," said Griflet. "Let me punish this knight who shames knighthood."

"You are young," said King Arthur. "Too young to face so violent and unscrupulous a foe."

"Let me show that my youth is no handicap," pleaded Griflet. "Let me redeem those shields and take them down from the tree."

King Arthur sighed. "It is your right to ask," he said. "I cannot deny you. Go, and my heart goes with you."

Next morning Griflet rode out to right the wrong done to knighthood. The next afternoon he came back bleeding and without his shield. The same thing happened to him that had happened to Sir Miles. Fortunately, his wounds were not fatal, but before they were healed, the king decided what must be done.

"I shall risk no more of my court," he said. "I shall deal with this black fellow myself. I will confront him not as his king but as another knight. I will wear a visor so he cannot see my face, and I will go forth at once. Fetch my war horse."

He had not ridden more than a mile or two when he saw something which outraged him. An elderly man was being attacked by three armed ruffians. He rode down upon the scoundrels, who fled in panic, and discovered that the man he had saved was none other than Merlin, the wise wonder-worker who had been his tutor.

"Merlin!" he exclaimed. "How lucky you are that I came in time to save your life."

"Thank you," said Merlin. "But," he added with a smile, "if I were really in danger I could always work a wonder and save myself. It is you, not I, who are on a most dangerous mission. Let me go with you."

They rode together until they came to the bridge. There, as Sir Miles's squire had told, were the black shield, the brass hammer, and the tree hung with the many shields of the knights that had been overcome.

"Look, Merlin!" exclaimed Arthur. "There must be a hundred shields on that tree!"

"You should be happy that yours is not one of them," said Merlin.

"And here is the sign that warns you to strike the shield only at the peril of your life. Discretion is the better part of valor. Perhaps you will be discreet enough to stop before you cross the bridge."

"Never!" said King Arthur. Without getting off his horse, he leaned over, picked up the hammer, and hit the shield so hard it rang like a dozen church bells.

The black knight came roaring like a black wind out of the castle, but King Arthur was ready. He met his opponent head on. There was a tremendous crash, the spears were splintered, and both men were thrown to the ground. Whipping out their swords, they flew at each other. They struck and parried, struck again and again, hacked and hewed, until their armor was battered and the men were breathless. They rested for a moment and then resumed the battle. The swords fell faster than ever until King Arthur struck the black knight's breastplate a tremendous blow and the royal blade broke in two.

"I have you now!" cried the black knight.

"Not yet!" cried the king, and flung himself against the other, carrying him to earth. They wrestled convulsively, thrashing the soil, until his opponent got his hands on King Arthur's throat. Up to this time Merlin had been standing grimly by. Now he spoke.

"Take your hand off that throat," he commanded, "or I will turn you into a toad. See whom you have dared to assault!"

Merlin lifted King Arthur's visor, and when the black knight saw the king's face, he fell to his knees.

"That is the proper position for you," said Merlin. "And, for fighting foul, you shall not get up until I see fit."

Merlin touched him on the shoulder and the black knight fell, seemingly lifeless, to the ground.

"That was not wise," said King Arthur, getting to his feet. "You have killed one who might have become the boldest of my knights."

"He will some day," said Merlin. "I did not kill him. He is not dead but sleeping. He will stay that way until you tell me to rouse him and bring him to your court."

"Meanwhile," said King Arthur, "I have lost that which once proclaimed me king. I have lost the magical sword I drew from the stone."

"We will find a better one," said Merlin, and led him out of the woods.

They rode until they came to a meadow where everything was

gold—gold buttercups, gold-centered daisies, gold lilies, gold laburnum trees in which goldfinches sang. And in the midst of this meadow was a broad lake a-dazzle with golden sunlight.

"Look at the center of the lake," said Merlin, "and tell me what you see."

"I see something I cannot believe I am seeing," said King Arthur. "An arm is being raised above the water. It is clad in pure white

silk interwoven with gold. And—wonder of wonders—it is holding a sword!"

"It is the sword that was made for you long before you were born," said Merlin. "It has a name: Excalibur, which means 'Cut-Through-Steel,' for there is no armor it cannot pierce. Here is a boat. Row out and take Excalibur."

They rowed to the center of the lake. King Arthur took the sword by the handle, and the arm disappeared under the water without a ripple. The king held the sword high over his head.

"I swear," said he, "never to use this blade except to right a wrong or save a life. I dedicate it to the service of chivalry and the cause of justice."

"So be it," said Merlin, as the two of them rode back to the king's court.

LANCELOT

...The Lady of Shalott

NUSUALLY tall, with dark hair that curled over his ears, and eyes that melted with tenderness or blazed with passion, he was a figure out of some romantic ballad. He had come to King Arthur's court later than most of the other knights and, since he was a foreigner, he had to explain himself.

"My name is Lancelot du Lac or, as you would say in this country, Lancelot of the Lake. I was called that because one day, when I was a babe, my mother left me for a moment on the bank of a lake and, while her back was turned, a water-witch rose from the lake and carried me away. She took me to a castle in the midst of the waters and there, where no man ever lived, I was reared. Now that I am grown to manhood, I have come to be admitted to your court and the honor of knighthood."

King Arthur looked favorably upon the youthful candidate and Queen Guenevere regarded him with an interest hard to hide. At that first meeting Lancelot knew his life would have a double devotion: loyalty to the king and love for the queen.

Lancelot passed all the tests without a sign of effort. He fought with knights who became his dearest friends; he overcame kings who were glad to be his allies. He was wooed by many women, but he did not yield to their endearments. He remained faithful to Queen Guenevere.

A year after he had been knighted, Lancelot was on a quest when he heard evil tidings. The queen had been kidnaped by a disloyal knight named Meleagans and was imprisoned in his castle. Lancelot turned back at once, gathered a few knights about him, and hurried to Meleagans' castle. There he and his followers were faced by a band twice as large as his own retinue. The battle was long and bitter. Spears were useless at such close quarters. Shields were pierced, armor was broken. Swords lashed and clashed until they snapped at the hilt. Men lay wounded and dying, but the queen was saved.

Lancelot had rescued her, but others brought her back to the court. Lancelot had been struck in the side and, since he was unable to ride, one of his men carried him, fainting, to the neighboring castle of Shalott. There he was put to bed, bandaged, and waited upon. It was the lord's daughter, Elaine, the lovely lily maid, who waited upon him, tended to his wounds, brought him food, and fell in love with him. It was a hopeless love, a love which was her doom, for Lancelot had love for only one woman: Guenevere. He had grown fond of Elaine and was grateful to her for her care. But when the wounds were healed, he thanked the lord of the castle, kissed Elaine, the lady of Shalott, on the brow, and resumed his quest.

The poet Tennyson retold the story of Elaine the fair, Elaine the lovable. She had dreamed of being Lancelot's bride or, if she could not be his wife, of following him like a slave through the world. Now, deserted and disconsolate, she sat in her tower. Day after day she waited for Lancelot, thinking that, somehow, he might return. In her imagination she saw him riding with the belt that held his sword thrown over one shoulder, his armor shining, and his silver bugle hanging at his side.

> All in the blue unclouded weather
> Thick-jewelled shone the saddle leather;
> The helmet and the helmet-feather
> Burned like one burning flame together
> As he rode down to Camelot,
>
> As often through the purple night,
> Below the starry clusters bright,
> Some bearded meteor, trailing light,
> Moves over still Shalott.

The days passed and still she sat, hoping against hope. When she realized he would never come back, she no longer wanted to live. She made up a song which she sang over and over. It began:

> Sweet is true love though given in vain, in vain;
> And sweet is death who puts an end to pain.
> I know not which is sweeter, no, not I.

Love, art thou sweet? Then death must bitter be.
Love, thou art bitter; sweet is death to me.
O Love, if death be sweeter, let me die.

She instructed that her body should be left on the bed on which
she died and placed on a barge. The boat should be covered in black

and pointed downstream toward Camelot. A lily should be placed in one hand, and in the other a letter telling of her love, a love that had no return. Then, when the orders had been given, her troubled heart stopped beating.

A little later Lancelot was standing at a palace window with the king and queen. The black barge had floated down the river and had stopped beneath them. Someone lifted the body of Elaine and carried it into the hall. Someone else handed the letter to King Arthur. He read it slowly while everyone wept. Then he spoke:

"Let the poor girl be buried, not meanly, but with royal ceremony. Let her tomb be costly and let her image and the story of her unhappy love be carved upon it in letters of azure and gold. Pray for her soul."

Lancelot bowed his head in grief. "Would that my mother had not left me on the bank but had drowned me in that lake," he moaned. "Would that some angel would seize me by the hair and bear me far away. Would that I had lived for something nobler than glory."

Gloriously, however, he lived. And nobly he died, for toward the end of his life, the champion of champions turned away from courts and combats. Lancelot of the Lake, once proud and powerful, became Brother Lancelot, lover not of one person but of all mankind

GALAHAD

...The Holy Grail

ING ARTHUR and his knights were assembled at the Round Table. Only one place stood empty: the Seat Perilous, so called because none but the absolutely pure dared sit in it without peril. It was always covered with a heavy cloth. An old hermit accompanied by a blond youth entered the hall.

"Your majesty," said the hermit, "I have brought one who is to sit in the Seat Perilous."

"You must be mad," said King Arthur. "Even the best of my knights is not without fault and none can claim to be pure enough to occupy that seat. Besides, who is this boy you have brought?"

"His name is Galahad, and he is a descendant of Joseph of Arimethea. It was Joseph of Arimethea who recovered the soldier's spear which pierced the side of the Saviour. He also was entrusted with the cup from which Jesus drank at the Last Supper and which caught His blood when the spear pierced His flesh on the cross. The cup, the Sangreal or Holy Grail, passed from generation to generation and was guarded by holy men. Years passed, centuries went by, and the guardians grew careless and profane. One day the Grail was no longer there. It is still on earth, but it cannot be seen except by one who is without sin and has never had a sinful thought. He who touches the Holy Grail can work miracles."

King Arthur looked at his knights, but none met his gaze.

"Of all quests, that would be the noblest and most difficult," he said. "But what has that to do with the boy? And why do you think he is fit to sit in the Seat Perilous?"

"Because I see what none of you has seen," said the hermit, and pointed to the chair. All eyes were turned his way as he lifted the heavy cloth and read what appeared on the seat in letters of gold: "This is the seat of Galahad, the pure in heart."

"He is to stay here until he wins the right to knighthood," said the hermit. "Then he is to go on his quest. He is to find the Holy Grail."

Galahad won his spurs within a year. Youngest of the knights, he was the most invincible and also the most chivalrous. He excelled at jousting, and his tourneying was a marvel to behold. He could unhorse any knight without injuring him; it was said that he was the only warrior that could win without wounding. When he set out on his quest, every knight at King Arthur's court pleaded to go with him.

"I thank you all," he said. "But this is something that has been foreordained, and it is something I must do alone."

Many were Galahad's triumphs as he encountered new adventures. He saved lords from undignified death and rescued ladies from cruel captivity. He stopped marauders from vandalism and made murderers repent. He overcame all adversaries and endured every hardship; his strength was as the strength of ten because his heart was pure.

One night he came to a castle where an old king lay grievously wounded near an altar.

"The wound," he told Galahad, "will never heal. It was caused by the spear that pierced our Saviour's side. Once I had it in my keeping, for I was brought up to be a holy man. But in my early manhood I sinned and the spear fell on me. Then it disappeared. The wound it caused crippled me, and though I am in constant pain, I cannot die. Only a miracle can save me."

"Do not lose faith," said Galahad. "Miracles have happened. Know that you must be strong to stand such suffering, and know that suffering must end. Believe it."

In the days that followed, Galahad found that he could not forget the king, the wound that would not heal, and the spear that had vanished. He went on, looking for a sign that would tell him his quest was not in vain. One evening he came to an abbey of white friars and, after spending the night there, he was shown the abbey's treasure. It was a white shield.

"It looks like any other shield," explained one of the friars, "but it has a strange history. It has been here since the abbey was founded —no one knows where it came from—and it has a curious power. Any knight who wears it, any knight except one, will be killed or badly maimed within three days. Many knights have laughed at the story and many have put on the shield and gone forth to battle. But they have all been found dead or disabled within three days, and their squires have brought the shield back. It stays here, waiting for the one who can wear it without hurt."

"You say that it is harmful to any knight, any knight except one," said Galahad. "Do you know who that one might be?"

The friar shook his head. "We do not know. It could be anyone. It could be you."

"It could be," said Galahad. "It could be a sign. Let me put it on."

The shield was brought. Galahad lifted it, and a dazzle of light filled the room. The walls glowed, the windows were illuminated with quivering colors, and on the white shield there appeared a shining golden cross. Its brightness increased as Galahad hung the shield around his neck and went on with his quest.

Something told him that what he was seeking was on this earth but not on land. He struck out toward the sea. When he reached the shore he found a ship without a crew but with all sails set for departure. Galahad entered the ship and it took off at once. It sailed smoothly, and when it reached the city of Sarras a silver table appeared in the center of the deck where nothing had stood before. It was a massive silver table, and on it was an object covered with a silk cloth. Galahad felt it must not be uncovered until the appointed moment. A man was standing on the dock, and Galahad asked him to help carry the table.

"Gladly would I help if I could," said the man. "But I have not walked for ten years except with crutches."

"Nevertheless," said Galahad, "come aboard and show your good will."

The man raised himself with difficulty, but as soon as he touched the table he straightened, his crutches fell, and he stood up stronger than he ever had been. News of this spread through the city. It reached the ruler who was confined to his bed by a disease no doctor could cure. He sent word that, if Galahad could restore him to health, he would surrender his greatest treasure, a spear which had mysterious powers but which no man could lift.

The table was carried to the ruler's bedside, and Galahad sensed this was the moment that had been appointed. He drew away the silk covering and an unearthly light began to glow. The light came from a cup on the table, a light that seemed liquid and turned from

gold to blood-red. Galahad clasped his hands and kneeled. He knew this was the precious vessel, the Holy Grail, and he knew he had come to the end of his quest. He bent in adoration while the Grail rose from the table, hovered above his head, and ascended to the 'skies. He did not notice the king who had left his bed and stood transfigured with joy.

"Stay here!" cried the ruler. "You have performed a miracle! Sarras is yours!"

"We have had a revelation," said Galahad. "I can only surmise what it may mean, but I know I am not meant to stay in Sarras. Something brought me here to further my mission. You spoke of a spear. If I can carry it, let me have it."

There was no need for Galahad to lift the sacred weapon. It floated toward him and fitted itself to his hand.

The journey back was swift. The ship was waiting, paths seemed to straighten themselves for his passing, nothing opposed his progress. He entered the old king's castle and, without a word, touched the king's wound with the point of the spear. The wound healed at once and the king enfolded Galahad in an embrace that was also a worship.

Galahad placed the spear on the altar. He had fulfilled his quest. He had seen the Holy Grail. He had earned the right to sit in the Seat Perilous. Pure and peerless, he was the fabled hero, the perfect knight.

BEAUMAINS

...*The Knightly Kitchen-Boy*

THERE WAS something mysterious about him. For one thing, he refused to give his name. Even when he stood before King Arthur and made his request, he said he was nameless. For another thing, his request was strange, especially for one so young, so handsome, and so strong that no knight could surpass him in brawn or beauty.

"I ask," he said, "to be given a place in the kitchen."

King Arthur was astonished.

"Have I heard you rightly?" he said. "You, a tall, strapping youth with the marks of noble bearing—you would be a scullion?"

"That is so," replied the youth. "I have taken an oath to serve my king in my own way. Let me assist the steward at his tasks. Let me help prepare the food. And let me have meat and drink for twelve months. Then, at the end of the year, I will ask two gifts."

"Assuredly, you shall have what you request. I have never denied meat and drink to anyone, not even to an enemy. I marvel that you do not ask for horse or armor or means of becoming a knight. But since you have taken an oath I will not tempt you to break it. As for a name, because you have such strong yet delicate hands, you shall be called Beaumains, which is French for Beautiful Hands. It is too bad that you have determined to use them in the scullery."

The youth who had acquired the name of Beaumains bowed and went to the kitchen without another word. He made friends with the serving boys at once. His manner was so warm that everyone welcomed his presence. He never complained or made the slightest demand. Yet, when there were tourneys or exhibits of sword-play, he would look longingly through the window, and when the knights contended with each other he would sacrifice a meal to attend the jousting.

One day when he was serving at the king's table, a maiden was ushered into the hall. She came with a petition and said the matter was urgent.

"Sire," she said. "There is a noble lady who is a prisoner in her own castle. A formidable villain has laid siege to the castle and threatens to take her if she does not yield to him. I beg that you appoint one of your knights to free the lady."

"Who may the lady be?" asked King Arthur.

"That I am not permitted to tell you, but the tyrant is known as Sir Ironside. It will require someone of great strength and stature to defeat him."

"If you cannot tell me her name," said King Arthur, "I cannot ask any of my knights to rescue her."

To everyone's surprise Beaumains addressed the king.

"Sire," he said, "have I permission to speak?" The king nodded. "I, too, was nameless," Beaumains continued. "I, too, know there are secrets that cannot be told except at the proper moment. I have served your majesty in the kitchen for twelve months, and now I ask the two gifts that were promised."

King Arthur smiled indulgently. "What are the two gifts?"

"The first gift is that you will grant me this quest: to go with this maiden," said Beaumains. "The second gift is that you make me a knight, so that I can challenge this presumptuous Ironside."

"I knew you would not spend your life in the kitchen," said King Arthur. "I knew you were meant to hold a sword in your hands instead of a spit. You shall have your two gifts. I shall make you a knight, and you shall go with this maiden on your quest."

The maiden drew herself up haughtily. "What!" she exclaimed. "Am I to have nothing better than a kitchen-boy!" Nevertheless, she waited while Beaumains was made a knight; she waited while he put on his armor and buckled on his sword. He made a resplendent figure as he mounted his horse and the two rode off together. She had to accept his company, but she never lost an opportunity to be rude to him.

"I should be ashamed to be riding alongside such as you. You do not carry the air of the court but the smell of the kitchen. Your business is with pots and pans, not with swords and spears. I would never have come to King Arthur's court had I thought I would have a cook as my companion!"

"Call me whatever you wish," said Beaumains. "Your words cannot drive me away. I have a task to perform and I will not leave you until I do what must be done."

"That is fine talk," said the maiden. "But all the kitchen food you ate and all the slops you drank will never give you strength enough to fight a warrior who claims he has never been defeated."

"We shall see," said Beaumains. "And I think I see my first test now."

What he saw was a knight surrounded by six robbers who were tying him to a tree and were about to take not only his armor but his life. Beaumains dashed at them, slew two of the robbers, wounded a third, while the other three took flight. When the knight was unbound, he begged Beaumains to stay at his castle and name a reward.

"God has given me strength to prove my knighthood," said Beaumains. "That is my reward. I thank you for your hospitable offer, but I cannot stay. I must follow my mission and this maiden."

The maiden showed no appreciation of what Beaumains had done. She was as discourteous as before.

"Don't expect praise from me," she said scornfully. "You were lucky that those men were cowards, fainthearted robbers, not bold knights. You are still a washer of dishes, a kitchen butcher who slaughters pigs. Wait until you are called on to slay a fighter."

Beaumains did not reply. Next morning when they came to a river she taunted him again.

"There is only one place to cross," she said, "and that is blocked by two mounted knights. Will you dare to challenge them, or will you go back to your dirty dishes?"

Instead of answering, Beaumains rushed at the foremost knight. They struggled in the water until Beaumains toppled his opponent who floundered in the stream. When the other knight attacked Beaumains he, too, was unhorsed and beaten.

"Once more luck was with you," said the disdainful maiden. "The horses stumbled on the slippery stones and their riders were helpless. I have yet to see a kitchen knave vanquish a knight in fair combat."

"Say what you will," said Beaumains. "I will not be angered. And I will not be deterred from my course."

They rode on in silence until they came within sight of a dark tower bearing a black banner. In front of the gate sat a huge knight in black armor on a black horse. The maiden seemed to relent.

"You have been fortunate so far," she said to Beaumains. "Do not trust to luck any further. Return before you are slain."

"It is kind of you to change your attitude," said Beaumains. "It is good to know you feel sorry for me. But though I am a kitchen-boy, I am not a coward. Let us see what this black knight may want."

The black knight showed what he wanted immediately.

"Give me your horse and your harness," he said, "and I will let you pass."

"Thank you for the offer," said Beaumains, "but I would like to keep my harness as well as my horse. I will pass. Stand out of my way."

The black knight came at him furiously. Beaumains waited until the knight was in reach of his spear. Then he thrust. The black knight's shield was shattered and the shaft of Beaumain's spear pierced his breastplate.

"He is wounded," said Beaumains, "but he will live. Let us carry him to the castle where his servants will take care of him."

For once the maiden had nothing to say. She even looked at Beaumains with something like respect and helped carry the stricken knight. Then they rode on. This time, however, instead of riding ahead of Beaumains she rode at his side.

The next day they were met by a knight clad in green who barred their way. "My brother, the black knight, must have asked payment to let you pass over his land. What payment will you make to pass through mine?"

"My mission does not include the making of payment," said Beaumains. "I can give nothing but courteous thanks."

"That is not enough," said the green knight, drawing his sword. Beaumains drew his and the two clashed against each other. The green knight was a hardened fighter but Beaumains was the more powerful. A mighty stroke on the helmet brought the green knight to his knees. He cried for mercy.

"What say you?" asked Beaumains of the maiden. "Should I grant his plea?"

The maiden was about to say something unpleasant, but she bit her tongue. "It is a strange thing when a knight-at-arms asks mercy of a kitchen-boy," she said. "And it is a stranger thing when a common kitchen-boy has the power of life and death over a noble. Strangest of all is that the kitchen-boy is the nobler of the two. Yes," she added, "spare him and be honored for it."

They stayed at the green knight's manor for the night, but Beaumains could not be persuaded to remain longer. Several times the maiden was on the point of mocking Beaumains, but whenever she looked at him she closed her lips. Toward the end of the day she spoke.

"Perhaps I have misjudged you," she said. "Perhaps you are not what you seem. In any event, you have proved valiant. Moreover, you never raised hand or voice against me when I was so rude. I am ashamed, and I ask forgiveness."

"There is nothing to forgive," said Beaumains. "And if there were, it is forgotten."

"You are generous," said the maiden. "You have done enough to prove your chivalry. I cannot let you do more, for if you do you shall surely die."

"What do you mean? What mystery are you concealing?"

"I told King Arthur only part of the story," said the maiden, "but you have earned the right to hear it all. My sister, the Lady Liones, is held prisoner in Castle Perilous by the wicked knight who calls himself Sir Ironside. I am Linet, her younger sister, and I was sent to persuade the king to send a company to her aid. When he refused and you volunteered, I was chagrined. I have acted hatefully. I cannot unsay the cruel things I said, but I hope to undo the wrong. This Sir Ironside is the most dangerous of knights. He has the strength of seven men. He is also the most treacherous, for he employs the methods of a murderer. When he cannot overcome his opponent in fair fight he uses means that are foul. If there is any danger of his losing a combat, five men spring out of hiding and strike down his adversary. Be warned, and leave before it is too late."

"I thank you for your thought, Linet," said Beaumains. "And I thank you for the warning. I will know how to deal with this Ironside who, in spite of his name, has a side that can—and will—be pierced."

When they came to Castle Perilous they saw the bodies of a dozen knights hung by the neck and dangling from the branches of an oak. They also saw a huge horn hanging from a tree. Linet begged him not to blow it, for it would call forth the murderous Ironside and his men.

"You have told me your name," said Beaumains. "It is time for me to tell you mine. I would not have you believe that I am, as you think, basely born. I swore to keep my name and origin secret until I had won my way to true knighthood. I wanted to win it not by favor but by merit, not by virtue of my heritage but by myself. So I put aside pride of ancestry and became a scullion. King Arthur had never seen me, for I was reared far from his court. Yet I am his nephew. My real name is Gareth, my father was King Lot, and my mother is King Arthur's sister."

Linet was about to curtsy, but he stopped her. "No more of this. No more words now, only deeds."

He blew the horn and Ironside appeared. He looked gigantic, violent, and invulnerable.

"Release the Lady Liones," cried Beaumains, "or do battle for her."

"You are a foolhardy youth," replied Ironside. "The lady is mine. Go now, or join the others who grace the tree."

"I will not go until I have lifted this shameful siege and have pledged my loyalty to the Lady Liones. Unless you free her, it will be you, not me, who will disgrace the tree."

"You think so?" bellowed Ironside. "Make ready to be killed."

This time Beaumains did not hold his ground, but hurled himself against the oncoming Ironside. The crash shook the earth. Both men were thrown from their horses and, holding their shields before them, rushed at each other. They fought for hours. They fought until their shields were broken and their armor battered. They fought until Beaumains broke his antagonist's sword and Ironside was helpless. His five villainous crew members were too cowed to do anything.

"I should let you live," said Beaumains, "for I am sick of battle and bloodshed. But you have sullied the name of knighthood and you should hang on the tree among your victims. Nevertheless, I will spare your life on one condition: that you ask mercy for the crimes you have committed, and ask it not of me but of King Arthur."

"I will do whatever you say," groaned the humiliated knight, and gave Beaumains the key to the castle.

When the gates were opened Beaumains marveled at what he saw. The lovely Lady Liones came down the stairs and his heart beat faster than it had in the most turbulent battle. She lowered her eyes as she stood before Beaumains and placed her hand in his.

"Welcome," she smiled. "Welcome to Castle Perilous."

THE CID

...The Will to Conquer

E WAS born in the eleventh century in a small town in Spain. His name was Rodrigo Diaz de Vivar, but by the time he was thirty he was known as the Cid, meaning "Lord" and signifying "Winner of Battles." The Spanish epic "El Cantar de Mio Cid" ("The Poem of My Lord") traces his career from that of a courtier to that of a hardened campaigner and conqueror.

Far from being a united nation, Spain at that time was divided into separate provinces at war with each other. The affairs of the country were still further complicated because large parts of Spain had been conquered by the Moors. Rodrigo was a native of Castile and was brought up in the Castilian court of Sancho the Second. Although he was a great favorite with the lords and ladies, formal receptions and courtly ceremonies bored him. He had served as a soldier under Sancho's father and he could not adjust himself to a life of inaction. One day he dared to address the king himself.

"I am grateful for all your majesty has done for me," he said. "But I can be of more use to you in another field."

"What field have you in mind?" asked the monarch.

"The battlefield," said Rodrigo. "Let me be your standard bearer. I will carry your banner through Spain."

He was as good as his word. He won battle after battle, campaign after campaign, until he was given the title of the Cid and Campeador, "The Champion." He seized the throne of León from Sancho's younger brother, Alphonso. When Sancho was killed during a siege, Alphonso became king of both Castile and León, and it seemed that the Cid's career was at an end. However, he proved to be as diplomatic as he was dauntless, and Alphonso welcomed him to his court. He remained there, sometimes as courtier, sometimes as conquerer, for ten years. When he married Jimena, Alphonso's niece, he was the second highest ranking man in the kingdom. He was also the proudest.

It was his pride that finally offended Alphonso. The Cid did not learn of this until, on his travels, he entered the city of Burgos. He was happy to be there, for it was near his birthplace. But, instead of the flags flying, the drums beating, and the popular acclaim he expected, there was silence. No one would speak to him. Astounded, he tried to get an answer from various citizens, but they turned away without a word. At last he teased a child into saying something.

Looking warily over her shoulder, she whispered, "The king."

"The king?" asked the Cid. "The king did what?"

"He warned us. He sent a letter. It said no one should take you into his house, or give you food, or talk to you."

For a moment he was stunned. He thought of punishing the king. He would desert him. He would fight against him. But this was unthinkable. Then he had a better idea. He would, on his own initiative, capture the stronghold of Valencia and present it to the king as a gift. But, when he had accomplished this, the king was not pleased. On the contrary, he was furious.

He stormed at the Cid. "What right had you to undertake a military project without our permission! You are too presumptuous, far too arrogant! I shall teach you a lesson. You are ordered into exile."

It was a bad time for the Cid. He considered withdrawing from fighting of every kind. But he could not give up the lure of combat and the will to conquer. Resentful, thirsting for revenge, he joined the king's enemies. He allied himself with the Moors, became their political adviser, and led them successfully on one expedition after another. He vanquished the counts of Aragón and Barcelona, and occupied their cities.

This period of revolt lasted a few years, but the Cid was not happy serving with the Moors. He rejoined his old companions, planned new campaigns, and was reconciled with Alphonso.

Once more he was in favor. His importance continued to grow. He conducted himself as though he were a royal personage and was treated accordingly. He wore a shirt looped with gold and silver, a

tunic of rich brocade, and a regal crimson robe bordered in ermine. His two daughters had been wed to nobles, but his sons-in-law had treated them badly. The Cid brought charges against the nobles, defeated them in a trial by combat, and had his daughters remarried to the princes of Aragón and Navarre. All those who had wronged him were severely penalized or imprisoned. He became undisputed ruler of Valencia.

The Cid died in his early fifties, fighting to the end. A legendary figure, a symbolic Castilian conqueror, arrogant and proud, he remains the great national hero of Spain.

JOAN OF ARC

... *The Warrior Maid*

HE WAS born Jeanne d'Arc in the little French village of Domremy. A peasant's daughter, she became known as Joan the Maid. Even as a child she was devout. Other girls danced the hours away, but Joan took as much pleasure going to church as others took going to fairs. At thirteen she began to have visions and hear voices. During the next five years the voices disclosed who they were. Joan knew them as Saint Catherine, Saint Margaret, and Saint Michael.

At that time France was not a nation but a battleground of warring parties. Taking advantage of the confusion, Henry VI of England claimed France as his own property and sent an army to take Orleans. The purpose of the campaign was to overrun all of France and drive the rightful ruler, young Charles the Dauphin, into exile. Joan's voices told her to expel the English and see that Charles the Dauphin was crowned king in the great cathedral at Reims.

Joan, who had never lifted a sword or held a lance, did not hesitate. She walked into the camp of Robert de Baudricourt, captain of a loyal troop, and told him about the voices.

"You must give me arms, a banner, and a horse," she said.

"Indeed?" said Robert. "And what will you do with them?"

"I will lead your troops to battle. I will lift the siege of Orleans. Then I will see that the Dauphin is anointed with the holy oil and crowned king in the great cathedral at Reims. That is the will of my master."

"What master gave you that command?" asked Robert sarcastically. "The king of France, perhaps?"

"The king of heaven," replied Joan.

Robert laughed. "Go home," he said good-naturedly. "Forget about leading troops. Go home and lead sheep to the pasture."

Joan was not discouraged. She returned to speak to Robert de Baudricourt again and again. Each time he shrugged her off, but not as brusquely as at first. The French were in a bad way; battles had been lost and they were facing new defeats. Finally he succumbed.

"Let her have a sword and a horse," he told one of his men. "Give her a little money so she can get what she needs to look more like a soldier. And see that she takes the right road to Chinon. She can't do us any harm, and if the soldiers believe in her, she may—I say *may* —do some good."

Discarding her peasant dress and putting on doublet, hose, and boots, Joan had a clerk write a letter to the king. She informed him that the time had come to save France and that she was on her way to help him do it.

News of Joan's strange story had reached Charles the Dauphin and he resolved to test her gift of vision. When she appeared he mingled with the courtiers and made one of his knights occupy the throne. Joan was not fooled. She was, however, puzzled when she came into the court.

"Where is the Dauphin?" she asked.

"You are in his presence," said the knight, drawing himself up majestically.

"You cannot trick me," said Joan. "I will know the Dauphin when I see him."

Quickly scanning the faces of the courtiers, Joan darted toward the Dauphin, who pulled away and pointed to the knight.

"Do you not recognize the king?" he said.

"I do, Sire," she answered. "You are he. I am God's messenger sent to see you crowned and to restore your kingdom to you."

The Dauphin was convinced. He had witnessed something no one had foreseen, something like a miracle. For a while he delayed giving her the power she desired, but at last he consented. She was allowed to go with the army for the relief of Orleans.

First, however, Joan had to be examined by the clergy, some of whom suspected that she might be a sorceress. There were three long weeks of questioning which failed to shake her.

"How do you know that your visions are not devils in disguise?" asked one of her questioners.

"By the same faith that tells me you are no devil," replied Joan.

"If God wills the English to be beaten, why do you need men-at-arms?" asked another.

"Because," said Joan, "the Lord wishes us to prove we love our country enough to defend it. We will fight and God will grant victory."

"You talk a great deal about your voices," said a third, a man who came from Limousin where everybody spoke with a thick accent. "In what language do the voices speak?"

"In a better language than yours," said Joan tartly.

"If you have been truly chosen by the saints," said the first, "give us a sign."

"I did not come to perform miracles," said Joan simply. "Let me go to Orleans and I will show you a sign that will convince everyone."

Finally they agreed that Joan deserved their trust, and she prepared to lift the siege of Orleans. Although she had never seen a battle, she was as expert in planning a campaign as a general who had devoted his whole life to studying the art of war. When she reached the Loire, her troops were drawn up on the banks of the river facing Orleans. Her captains advised transferring the troops to a more favorable position because the wind was blowing so fiercely that no boats could cross. Joan did not agree.

"We will stay and attack from here," she said.

"It is the worst place," said her captains.

"The worst place is the best for us," said Joan. "The English will never expect us to cross here. But cross we will."

At that moment the wind changed. The boats were loaded with men and provisions and soon Joan's army stood before Orleans. She was the first to plant a scaling ladder against the wall and she was the first to mount the battlements. An arrow stuck her in the shoulder, but she pulled it out with her own hands. "Fight on!" she cried. "The place is ours!"

As always she was right. The English could not resist her. They felt they were fighting a force out of this world. Joan went on to take town after town from the invaders. A few weeks after the triumph at Orleans, the prophecy of her voices was fulfilled when she stood beside the Dauphin at Reims and saw him crowned king.

In spite of Joan's victories, the war went on. One of the most powerful French factions, the Burgundians, aided the English and occupied the town of Compiègne. When Joan went to the aid of the city there was treachery and she was taken prisoner. Her army was

demoralized. No attempt was made to rescue her. The Dauphin whom Joan had helped to become king did not even offer to ransom her. The Burgundians sold her to the English. Although the English had threatened to execute Joan as a witch, they preferred to ruin her in the eyes of those who worshiped her, discredit the king, and destroy her influence once and for all. They turned her over to a court of inquiry.

It was an ecclesiastical court, but it was dominated by the English, the Burgundians, and a few false Frenchmen. The purpose of the court was to prove that Joan was allied with the powers of evil. She was charged with twelve counts, all of them damaging to her reputation. Among other things, she was accused of sorcery, of lying about her visions and her voices, of refusing to wear proper womanly dress and clothing herself like a man, of being stubborn, proud, and scornful of her superiors. Worst of all, she was denounced for claiming that she was responsible only to God and not to the church, a declaration that the churchmen considered worse than blasphemy.

The trial dragged on until, weakened after endless questioning and threatened with torture, she signed a paper without really understanding what she was admitting. A few days later, she said her voices had again spoken to her, and she thereupon repudiated her so-called "confession."

"They told me that I had committed a great sin when I signed a paper in order to live," she said. "They told me I must not lose my soul in order to save my life." She said she feared falsehood more than death.

That was the end. The charges were upheld by the court. She was condemned as a heretic and burned at the stake. As the flames went up, she heard her voices comforting her, and, with a cry of "Jesus!" she died.

Afterward, efforts were made to shift the blame for the tragedy. The French blamed the English, the English blamed the French. King Charles waited fifteen years before he instituted a trial to clear Joan's name and (equally important to him) clear his own name for having done nothing to save her. The proceedings were long and complicated; twenty-five years elapsed before she was declared innocent and established as a martyr. Her name became a byword for courage and piety.

Four hundred and ninety years after her death the peasant maid of Domremy was canonized as Saint Joan.

AUCASSIN AND NICOLETTE

...*Their Difficult Romance*

NE OF the most suspenseful of all love stories was composed by an unknown French poet more than seven hundred years ago. The tale is said to have had its origin in Arabia, but the setting is that part of France known as Provence.

Aucassin was the only son of the combative Count of Beaucaire, but he did not inherit any of his father's warlike spirit. He refused to bear arms, he took no part in tournaments, he did not even care for hunting. He was a dreamer, a dreamer who dreamed of only one thing: his beloved Nicolette.

His father was exasperated. "Bad enough that you do not act like a man," he said angrily. "But that you should fall in love with a worthless girl is beyond reason! There are plenty of titled ladies who might be your bride; there is no excuse for you to moon over a slave."

"She is not a slave!" cried Aucassin.

"She is little better—she is a nobody. My vassal bought her from pirates when she was a child. He has brought her up to do household work and marry some good farmer. Be sensible and forget her."

"I would do almost anything to please my father, but that is something I cannot do," said Aucassin. "Her name is always on my lips, her laughter is always in my mind, her love is always in my heart. I cannot think of any bride but Nicolette."

"I will see to it that you never look at her again," said his father, grimly. "Then you will forget her." He summoned his vassal and gave strict orders.

"Your Nicolette is the cause of my son acting so badly," said the count. "He will never be a knight until she is removed from his presence. Send her far away or lock her up—I do not care which, so long as he no longer sees her."

The vassal did as he was told. He put Nicolette in the tower room of his house and got an old woman to watch over her and bring her food. The door was locked. What fresh air there was came in through a window looking on a garden. For a while people were surprised at Nicolette's disappearance. Some said that she had been sent out of the country; others said that the count had put her to death. After a while she was forgotten by everyone—everyone except Aucassin.

Aucassin, distracted, went from place to place looking for his beloved Nicolette. When he could find no trace of her, he threw himself, heartbroken, on his bed and wept bitterly. There his father found him. He spoke reproachfully.

"You should be ashamed to shed such unmanly tears at any time, especially at a time like this. The Count of Valence is at our gates. His pikemen and horsemen are drawn up in front of the town. Our own knights are on the battlements of the castle. We need every man. Get up and arm yourself. Mount your horse. You are strong, and when the men see you among them they will fight harder to defend their land—which is also yours. Fight for it!"

"God forbid that I should kill anyone," replied Aucassin. "The Count of Valence means nothing to me. Nor does the castle. Nor the country. Let him have it. I do not care. The only thing I care about is Nicolette. Let me have her."

"Never," said his father. "I would rather lose all I have rather than let you marry a low-class servant."

Without another word he turned to leave. Aucassin stood up and stopped him.

"Father," he said. "I will make a bargain with you."

"What talk is this?" said his father. "What kind of bargain?"

"It is this," said Aucassin. "I will put on armor; I will fight. And if God brings me safely back, will you let me see Nicolette again, speak with her, and give her a loving kiss?"

"It is a bargain," said his father. "You have my word on it."

It was a happy Aucassin who clad himself in battle-gear. He put on his chain-mail coat, laced the helmet on his head, fastened his gold-hilted sword at his side, and gripped his lance. Mounting his charger he led the men against the enemy. Careless of danger, he rode recklessly. He gave no thought to the enemy or how the battle was to be fought. He thought only of victory and what his father had promised.

Before he could strike a blow, he found himself surrounded and captured. The enemy took his lance and shield and were about to do away with him when Aucassin woke to reality.

If I die I will never see Nicolette. That must not be, he thought. "I still have my sword," he cried.

In a flash he swung the blade about him, cutting through everything in his path, striking down a dozen knights until he came to the Count of Valence. He struck again so fiercely that the count was tumbled to the ground. Aucassin led him captive to his father.

"Here, father, is your enemy," said Aucassin. "Now perform your part of the bargain."

"What bargain?" said his father.

"You know very well," said Aucassin. "The promise that, if God brought me safely back, you would let me see Nicolette again, speak with her, and give her a loving kiss."

"It was a silly bargain," said his father. "No one could take it seriously. As for that girl, were she before me, I would condemn her to the fire."

"Do you mean that?" said Aucassin incredulously.

"I do," said his father.

Aucassin turned to the Count of Valence. "You are my father's enemy. You are also my prisoner, and I can do with you as I wish. I will set you free if you promise to cease making war and cease having anything to do with my father."

The Count of Valence promised and, pledging his troth, rode through the gates of the city with Aucassin at his side.

Aucassin's father was more furious than ever. He ordered his men to pursue Aucassin, to seize him and throw him into a dungeon deep below the earth. There Aucassin lay, with only one small window to let in light, sad and sick at heart for Nicolette.

Nicolette, meanwhile, languished in her tower. It was the month of May and she lay sleepless, watching the moon through the casement, listening to the singing of a nightingale. The nightingale's song was so full of the pain and ecstasy of love that Nicolette could not bear to listen. Nor could she remain any longer in confinement. Knowing that the old woman was asleep behind the locked door, she rose, wrapped herself in a mantle, and knotted the bedsheets together to make a long rope. Fastening one end of the rope to the window frame, she slipped down into the garden. She took her skirt in both hands, tucking it up against the dew thick on the grass, and ran through the gate. Her steps were so light that she scarcely bruised the daisies as she ran over them.

Once in the street she walked close to the sides of houses, keeping within the shadows. Passing the dungeon in which Aucassin was kept, she heard weeping and stopped to investigate. She thought she recognized her lover's voice and, bending down, she whispered, "Dear Aucassin, you have suffered too long for someone who is not worthy of you. Your father will never allow us to wed, and I will not allow you to remain in this dark dungeon because of me. I am going to some other place. I do not know where, I only know it will be far away from here."

Cutting a lock of her golden hair, she kissed it, inserted it between the bars and, as Aucassin put it next to his heart, she vanished.

Nicolette made her way through treacherous alleys, across moats, over fences, out of the city until, her feet bleeding and her body bruised, she came to a forest. She was afraid of beasts and snakes, but she feared wild things less than she feared men who might find her and drag her back to prison. Too tired to worry, she fell asleep.

She was wakened by the song of birds and the sound of laughter. A few shepherds had spread their cloaks on the grass near a spring and were passing bread and wine to each other.

"God bless you," she said.

"God bless you, too," they replied. "What brings you here?"

"A heavy heart," she answered. "But you could help me. You all know Aucassin, the count's son. If you should see him, give him a message from me. Tell him that there is a quarry for his hunting in this forest. Tell him that he will have no trouble catching it, and when he has caught it, he should not exchange it for a hundred gold marks."

"I will tell him," said one of the shepherds. "It is a jesting message, for there is no beast in these woods that is worth a handful of copper pennies, let alone a hundred gold marks."

"Tell him, anyway," said Nicolette, and, bidding them farewell, went deeper into the forest. There she made herself a little lodge, a bower of large leaves and lilies of the field, and waited in it.

Meanwhile the news spread that Nicolette had disappeared. Again the rumors flew through the city. Some said that she had escaped, others said that she had been killed. The Count of Beaucaire heard the news with great pleasure. He released his son and sent agents to various lords inviting them to bring their daughters and join his

son at a royal feasting. Aucassin had no heart for festivities. While preparations were being made, he mounted his horse and rode off. Alone with his grief, he let his horse wander aimlessly. Presently he entered the forest and there, lunching on the grass, were the shepherds that had talked with Nicolette. One of them was singing, but he stopped.

"God bless you," said Aucassin.

"God bless you, too," they replied.

"Will you continue with your song? I would like to hear the rest of it!"

"You are Lord Aucassin," said the singing shepherd, "and our songs are too common for you. Instead, I will tell you a story. The other day as we were breaking our fast, a young maid came by. She looked like a maid, but she may have been a fairy. She was so lovely she filled these shade-hung woods with light. She gave us a message—and it was a message for you. She said that there was a quarry for your hunting in this forest. She said, moreover, that you would have no trouble catching it, and when you have caught it, you should not exchange it for a hundred gold marks."

"Thank you," said Aucassin. "It is a marvelous message."

"I am glad," said the shepherd. "Good hunting."

Aucassin put spurs to his horse and dashed into the woods. All day he charged through thickets, across streams, into groves, without sighting his quarry. His clothes were torn by thorns and spines; he was bleeding from countless scratches. But he never stopped to rest. It was nightfall before he found the bower and within it his quarry, the lovely Nicolette. They fell into each other's arms, embraced closely, and kissed a thousand times. They talked endlessly of their joy; then they held each other for hours without uttering a word.

In the morning Nicolette sighed and said, "We cannot remain here. Missing you, your father will send out a searching party. We will be found, and then—" She shuddered.

"You are right," said Aucassin. "We must go at once. But where?"

"My love," said Nicolette. "It does not matter where we go. France or Italy, town or country, land or sea, nothing matters as long as I am with you."

So, setting her in front of him, Aucassin mounted his horse and, holding her fast, drove toward the shore. A merchant ship was being loaded, and the captain agreed to take them along. They were out in the open sea only a few hours when a violent storm drove them far from their destination. Fortunately, the vessel landed intact in the kingdom of Torelore. It was a madcap country—the king and queen were both somewhat daft—but the lovers were welcomed. They enjoyed themselves thoroughly until one day a fleet of Saracens took over the port, besieged the city, stormed the castle, and bound most of the men and women in captivity. Aucassin was put on one ship and Nicolette on another.

It was the season for storms, and once again the vessels were thrown off course. Nicolette's ship was driven toward the coast of Carthage, while Aucassin's, its sails gone and its mast broken, drifted to the coast of France near the castle of Beaucaire. When he landed, he learned that his father had died and that he was now ruler of the country. He should have rejoiced, yet, though he had honor and power, his heart was heavy. What he had gained meant nothing, for he had lost what he held dearest: his one and only love.

The ship which carried Nicolette weathered the storm and brought her to Carthage. When she came on shore the people were so struck by her grace and beauty that they brought her to the palace. Everything seemed strangely familiar to her—the streets, the houses, the flowering trees, the costumes—it was as if she knew them all. When she stood before the king of Carthage she trembled with an excitement she could not suppress. He stared at her.

"Do not be frightened," said the king. "There is something about you that moves me. Tell me who you are."

"Alas, your majesty," replied Nicolette. "I do not rightly know who I am. I only know that when I was a child fifteen years ago I was stolen from my home and sold in France to a vassal of the Count of Beaucaire."

"Fifteen years ago!" exclaimed the king. "It fits! I knew there was something about you that I seemed to recognize. I was not too sure. Now I know for certain. You are my lost daughter, the child who was stolen fifteen years ago."

Never had there been such rejoicing. All Carthage went on holiday. Nicolette was acclaimed as a perfect princess and clad in the most radiant clothes. A string of precious pearls was placed around her ivory neck.

"We must find a proper husband for you, my dear," said the king. "There are princes and even kings who will be happy to ask for your hand."

"I am your daughter and should do as you say," said Nicolette. "But there is only one husband for me. No matter where he may be, no matter how long it takes, I must find him."

Nicolette knew what she must do. One night she bound up her hair, covered it with a cap, stained her face, put on doublet and hose, and disguised herself as a minstrel. Then, carrying a viol, she slipped away and boarded a ship sailing for France. Once there, she traveled through the villages of Provence seeking news of Aucassin. When she reached Beaucaire she learned that, his father having died, Aucassin was now ruler. Uncertain that he still loved her, the disguised Nicolette appeared one day while Aucassin sat in a garden with friends.

"You are welcome, minstrel," said Aucassin. "Sing something, something sad to suit my mood."

"It will be sad yet sweet," said Nicolette, "for it will be a song of love."

So Nicolette sang about the devotion of two young lovers, how the youth had been punished because of his love, how his beloved had escaped from her prison, how they had been reunited and then separated, how she had found herself in Carthage and was recognized as the king's daughter, how her father wanted her to marry some king or caliph, but that she would never be wife to anyone except the man she had always loved.

"That is my song and my story!" cried Aucassin. "And do you know the girl whose ballad you have just sung?"

"I know her well," said Nicolette. "So well, in fact, that I can persuade her to present herself to you today."

"If you only could!" sighed Aucassin. "But that is impossible."

"Nothing is impossible, my lord," said Nicolette and, smiling, left the garden. In her old home, the house of the vassal, she removed the stain from her face, let down her hair, shed the minstrel's garb, put on a silk gown she had concealed, and fastened the string of pearls around her neck.

When she appeared before Aucassin, his sadness suddenly fell away, his face grew radiant, he sprang to his feet, and she rushed into his arms.

With this happiest of endings, the unknown twelfth-century poet ended his romance:

> Thus, the poem you have heard
> Ends with the true lovers' word.
> 'Spite of sorrow, sob and sigh,
> Love like theirs will never die.
> Never will the world forget
> Aucassin and Nicolette.

THE LITTLE JUGGLER

...And the Virgin

 ONG AGO in France there was a poor young fellow who had only one talent: he could juggle. Not great or famous enough to perform in the big cities, he made some sort of living going about the countryside entertaining farmers, their wives, and their children at country fairs. There he would do his turn, balance a few cups and saucers on a stick, do a little dance while carrying a bowl full of water on his head, make things disappear, and keep half a dozen balls in the air at one time.

It was not an easy life and, more often than not, little money was forthcoming. Time and again he had to go from place to place with barely enough food to keep himself alive. The winters were the worst. There were no fairs and no audiences; the roads were icy; freezing winds blew through his thin and shabby clothes. He never complained. "God is good," he told himself when someone gave him a bit of bread and meat or put him up for the night. "The blessed Virgin sees all. She will take care of me." He not only crossed himself whenever he passed a roadside shrine but stopped and said a part of a psalm he had learned and which he never varied. "The Lord is my shepherd; I shall not want. He maketh me to lie down in green pastures"—he sometimes shivered, shaking off snow when he said this, but he went on—"He leadeth me beside the still waters. He restoreth my soul. Surely goodness and mercy shall follow me all the days of my life. And I will dwell in the house of the Lord for ever."

One day when he finished saying these words, he realized he was standing in front of a monastery. "Why," he said to himself, as though he had never seen a monastery before, "this *is* the house of the Lord—at least it is one of His houses. How wonderful would it be if I could really dwell in the Lord's house."

Emboldened by the thought, he knocked on the door. A monk opened it and, thinking the juggler was a beggar, asked him to wait while he brought him a bowl of milk.

"It is good of you," said the juggler. "But I am more in need of another kind of food. I need to dwell in the house of the Lord—if not for ever, at least as long as He will permit. May I come in?"

"This house is dedicated to the worship of the blessed Virgin. We cannot deny strangers temporary lodging. But to remain with us—What can you do?"

"Not much," sighed the juggler. "I can balance cups and saucers on a stick, do a little dance while carrying a bowl full of water on my head, make things disappear, and keep a dozen balls in the air at one time. I can also say my prayers standing on my head. These things, I am afraid, are not what is required of one who would like to lead a spiritual life. But I can learn. I am devoted to the blessed Virgin and I would serve her night and day. Tell me what is to be done and I will do it."

The monk smiled and led him to the abbot. The abbot sympathized with the poor juggler and, touched by his desire to lead another life, admitted him to the monastery. There the juggler performed the lowliest tasks. Nothing was too much or too mean for him. He washed the floors, he cleaned the cells, he dusted the pews, he weeded the garden, he dug the carrots, he peeled the potatoes, he scrubbed the pots and polished the copper pans. He could not do enough, but it never seemed enough for him.

What am I doing to serve the blessed Virgin? he thought. What can I do to show her the depth of my devotion? The others glorify her by composing hymns in her honor, or inscribing on vellum the story of her virtues, or decorating the chapel, or writing books of prayers, or painting the margins of the pages with delicate designs in the fairest colors brightened with gold. All the others praise her and sing songs to please her. But what am I doing for her pleasure?

Day after day this thought plagued him. It never let him alone. Then one night he had a dream, a dream that told him what to do. The other monks had never paid any attention to him when he went about his work. Now they began to notice a change in him. He, who had been sad and lonely, was always smiling. Instead of being slow, his walk was brisk. He said, "*Good* morning," and made it sound

as if every morning were good. Then they noticed something else. They noticed that, whenever the chapel was empty, he would go there and remain for what seemed a particularly long period of prayer. They wondered, moreover, why he hurried through his work and ran to the chapel whenever there was the least opportunity.

Finally the abbot called a few of the senior monks. "It would be not only rude but wrong to intrude upon a brother's privacy, especially when he is at prayer. But I confess his behavior puzzles me. I think we have a right to clear our minds of confusion. Without being seen we should see what is happening. We could open the chapel door the merest slit. That should be sufficient."

The next time the little juggler disappeared, the abbot and two of the elder monks went to the chapel, barely opened the door, and looked through the crack. They saw the juggler standing in front of the statue of the blessed Virgin doing the things he always did to please audiences. He balanced a few cups and saucers on a stick, he did a little dance while carrying a bowl full of water on his head, he made things disappear, and he kept half a dozen balls in the air.

The abbot flung the door wide open. "Sacrilege!" he cried. "An insult to the blessed Virgin! To think we have given shelter to a common clown! You shall be thrown out!" He started toward the juggler who was crouching in fright.

At that moment the blessed Virgin came down from her altar, smiled, and, with a simple gesture, wiped the perspiration from the little juggler's brow.

ROBERT OF SICILY

... The Proudest King

 NE OF the favorite stories of the fourteenth century was about pride, which, according to the medieval preachers, headed the list of the Seven Deadly Sins. Told originally in Latin, the story has often been retold, notably by Longfellow in a long narrative poem. All the versions agree that pride and conceit are dangerous and that the man who is too proud will be humbled.

This, then, is the story of Robert of Sicily, the proudest monarch ever born. He felt there was good reason for his pride. His family was not only fabulously rich but famous. One of his two brothers was Emperor of Germany, the other was the Pope in Rome. He himself ruled supremely and sternly over the whole island of Sicily. "The crown," he liked to say, "is the symbol of nobility, but it is I who ennoble the crown."

One evening while he sat in his private bejeweled chapel listening with half a mind on the vesper hymn and the more important half on plans for increasing his power, he happened to hear the Latin words of the service. *"Deposuit pontentes de sede, et exaltavit humiles,"* chanted the priests. He had never noticed the phrase before.

"What does it mean?" he asked.

"It says," replied his chief councilor, "that He, meaning the Almighty Power, has put down the mighty from their seat, and has exalted the humble."

"That is a treasonable utterance," said King Robert darkly. "It is a good thing that it is murmured only in Latin and sung only by priests. It is also a foolish utterance, for there is no power that can unseat me. I sit secure on my throne. And I always will." He yawned

—music usually made him drowsy; the chapel was warm, the candle light caused his eyelids to droop. He nodded, and fell asleep.

When he woke the chapel was empty. The priests had gone; his councilor was no longer at his side; the candles had guttered out. Groping in the dark, he called for his servitors and beat on the door for the sexton.

"Where is everyone?" he shouted angrily. "There are punishments for leaving the body of the king unprotected!"

Finally the sexton was aroused. "And who are you," he said scornfully, "to make such a racket! Have you no respect for the church! Who *are* you?"

"I am your king, as you will see if you lift your lantern! And you will pay for this!"

"The king?" sneered the sexton, flashing the lantern about him. "You are either a witless beggar who chanced to sleep over his prayers or—worse—a thief who has come to steal the candlesticks from the altar. Out with you!" And he pushed the king through the doors of the church into the street.

It was a quiet night with a brilliant moon, and there was no one in sight. Robert, king of Sicily, picked himself up from the pavement and saw his reflection in a window. He could not believe what he saw. He saw himself clad in rags; he had no hat; his cloak was nothing but tatters. Shivering with cold and hot with fury, he ran to the palace and, elbowing aside everyone who tried to stop him, thrust himself before the throne.

For a moment he was speechless. There sat another king, clad in the royal regalia, wearing his crown, and even looking like him. It was an Angel who had taken his place. Unaware of this, Robert of Sicily stood aghast. Then he regained his voice.

"What does this mean?" he exclaimed. "Who is responsible for this mockery?"

"I am," said the figure on the throne. "And who are you?"

"You know well enough who I am!" retorted Robert violently. "I am Robert, king of Sicily, and you are an imposter."

"You neither look nor act like a king, my poor man," said the Angel quietly. "Let me tell you what you are. You are a fool. Not a very merry fool, and I am afraid that you would have trouble playing the jester at any court. But I am sorry for you, and I will help you. I shall let you stay here and become *my* fool. Then, since the fool considers himself a king, he must have a councilor. You shall have an ape to give you counsel as well as companionship.

And now, unless you can think of a better jest, you may leave us."

Staggering with exasperation, Robert started to mount the steps of the throne, but two of his own guards seized him. The struggle was short, and he was half pushed, half pulled down the stairs into a small room under the kitchen. There his clothes were removed, and, though he kicked and screamed in a most unroyal rage, a jester's suit was put on him. "Long live the king!" laughed the servants as they thrust a clown's bladder in his hand and left him.

The next morning he woke to find a pewter plate with some scraps of food and, in the opposite corner, a monkey dressed as he was, grotesquely equipped with cap and bells.

"Well," said the Angel, after Robert was summoned to the throne-room, "who are you today?"

"The same as I was yesterday," said Robert haughtily. "I am the king!"

"Alas, you are still a fool," said the Angel sadly, "a fool who does not know how foolish he is. We will have to wait until your folly is less arrogant."

It was a seemingly endless wait. Under the Angel's influence the country grew increasingly prosperous. The crops were bountiful, and the people, free of Robert's iron rule, relaxed into undisturbed happiness. Even the volcanic Mount Etna stopped fuming and was quiet. Never had Sicily been so peaceful, and never had the deposed Robert been so bitter.

Three years passed, but Robert's heart was still hard with pride and hatred. The courtiers jeered at the glum and tight-lipped jester and his ape. "Why does the king keep the sour-faced fool?" they said. "A jester who cannot jest is his own bad joke." During those years, whenever the Angel would ask him, "Fool, are you still proud of yourself?" the answer was always the same. "Why not? A noble must be proud—and I am the king!"

At the end of three years the Pope summoned his brothers to visit him in Rome. The Angel brought along a resplendent retinue. Robed in silver, with armor that flashed the sun back at itself, he rode at the head of the lordly procession. In the rear, on a seedy nag, was the dismal fool with his monkey, a miserable imitation of himself, perched on his shoulder. As they passed through town after town, the inhabitants, thinking that the fool was playing a heart-sick role, laughed and applauded him, while Robert's scowl grew blacker and blacker.

The Swiss Guard saluted, the trumpets sounded a fanfare, and the cannons boomed a welcome as the Angel and his company neared the basilica of Saint Peter. Everything proceeded with pomp and dignity until the Pope held his reception. Then Robert burst through the assemblage and cried, "Look! I am your brother Robert, king of Sicily! This man is a fraud, an imposter who has disguised himself to look like me! Surely you must know your own brother!"

The Pope turned to the Angel for an explanation, but the Angel only shook his head and smiled. The poor fellow is demented,

thought the Pope. Then, with a desperate demand, Robert appealed to his other brother, the Emperor of Germany. "Look again!" he cried, and this time it was a real cry, for there were tears in his voice. "Something inside you must tell you we are kin! It is only my garb that has changed, not me myself! If a brother cannot tell his own brother, surely a king must recognize another king!"

The Emperor of Germany was perplexed and a little annoyed. "Every country has its own customs," he said to the Angel. "But it would never occur to me to keep a madman for my fool."

The visit was over. The Pope had bestowed his blessing upon everyone, even upon the fool who acted like a madman. The Emperor returned to the north, and the Angel took his company south through Italy. It was a solemn journey, and Robert finally was affected by the solemnity. He ceased to scowl. From time to time he raised his eyes, and there was no anger in them. Once he patted the monkey on his shoulder, and the servitors thought he smiled.

The day after they arrived in Sicily the Angel sent for him. "Do you still believe a fool is fit to be king?" he inquired.

"You know best," replied Robert, and added, "my lord."

"But it is you who must say," gently insisted the Angel. "Are you a king? One who is proud to wear a crown?"

"I am a fool," said Robert humbly. "I did not know that a man should be proud of what he does, not of what he wears, even if it is a crown."

"You have been blest with more than a benediction," said the Angel. "You have been blessed with knowledge. Before this, you had my pity; now you have my faith. Look about you."

He looked, but the Angel was gone. He was alone in the throne room. The ermine robe was draped over his shoulders; the crown was on his head. Strains of music came from the church. Priests were chanting: "He has put down the mighty from their seat, and has exalted the humble." He repeated the words himself and felt the weight of every syllable.

When his courtiers entered, they found King Robert kneeling, at prayer. His crown had been discarded. Instead, a golden light from some high window illumined his brow.

THE TAILOR'S APPRENTICE

... And the Bear

HE TOWN of Wolfach lies in the midst of the Black Forest of Germany, and in the town of Wolfach lived a tailor's young apprentice. He had—according to the usual formula—been cheated out of his inheritance by his older brothers. A pair of scissors, a piece of rope, and a violin were all that was left to him. Nevertheless, the boy was not downhearted.

"It isn't much," he said. "But with these three things I'll make my fortune."

It was a long time before he could put the three things to any use. No one trusted him to cut a yard of linen by himself; no one stopped to listen to his five-finger exercises; and the best use for the rope seemed to be to hang himself. After three years of wandering he had gained nothing—nothing except a pocketful of smooth pebbles which (he liked to pretend) felt like money.

Finally he came to a country where there was—as there usually is —a princess who had vowed she would give her hand in marriage only to the one who would rid her land of a scourge worse than a dozen dragons. This was an enormous bear which had ravaged the countryside and was beginning to invade the capital itself. This bear was so large that its skin would have supplied a whole regiment with fur coats; its teeth were so pointed that one bite did the work of twenty saws; its claws were so long and sharp that when it ran through a field it was as if an army of mowers had passed. A thousand suitors had wooed the princess only to scurry away at the first sight of the monster, while thirty-three more foolhardy spirits had remained for a second glimpse.

Seeing that his three possessions were secure, the tailor's lad walked boldly to the edge of the forest where the bear lurked. Gathering a pocketful of filberts, he began to eat them. Soon a crashing of boughs, as though a herd of elephants were stampeding, warned him that the bear was near. The boy continued to munch filberts. The bear plunged nearer. Now it was within twenty yards of its victim, now its rank breath was on the nape of the lad's neck. The huge jaws opened, but something—surprise or curiosity—kept them open.

"What are you doing?" it asked.

"Eating filberts," replied the tailor's apprentice. "Have some?" And, putting his hand in another pocket, he gave the bear a fistful of pebbles.

The bear bit and bit, but he could make no dent in the stones.

"How do you crack them?" asked the bear. "I don't seem able to do it."

"Any child knows how," answered the lad. "Just grind your teeth a little harder and you'll see."

The bear ground and ground until his teeth were worn down to the gums, whereupon the boy took out his fiddle.

"What are you going to do now?" asked the bear.

"Play something on the violin," answered the lad. "I always have a little music after my meals." And he played "Silent Night" six times without stopping.

"That's better than nuts," said the bear. "Tell me, is it hard to learn?"

"Child's play," answered the tailor's apprentice. "First you put a finger on this string, then another on the second, then you draw your bow across, and that's all there is to it."

"It seems easy," nodded the bear, "and it would be nice to play myself to sleep on winter nights. Could you give me lessons?"

"Gladly," responded the boy, "and it won't take long. But before we begin, I'll have to cut your nails; otherwise you'll snap the strings." And, with his scissors, he cut the sword-like claws down to the soft flesh. Then the lad got on his knees and put his palms together.

"And what are you doing now?" asked the bear.

"Praying," answered the lad. "Before starting anything I always pray for success—and it never fails."

"It sounds sensible," murmured the bear. "I'll do it, too," and, lumbering to his knees, the great bear lifted his paws together.

Immediately, the tailor's apprentice whipped out his rope and bound the monstrous paws. With its teeth useless, claws clipped, and crushing power gone, the creature was helpless. Leading it back to the palace, the tailor's apprentice won the applause of the people, the hand of the princess, and, in a few years, the throne of two countries.

And, concludes the Wolfachian, whoever doesn't believe me must pay me a dollar.

THE ROBBER BARON

... And the Bat

A BAND of robber barons had come back with another rich haul of money and merchandise. The banquet that celebrated the occasion was drawing to a close. Men with bloodshot eyes sprawled over benches, their women lolled heavily in their seats. Hohlmund, chief of the robber barons, swayed to his feet. "Much-lauded ladies"—whereat the ruffians laughed—"and many-ladied lords"—here the women tittered at the tasteless joke—"as a grand finale to the festivities, I present the wildest animal that ever roamed the Rhineland. Ho, there! Bring in the bat!"

The women shrank back as the door opened and two servants brought in a chained creature. His hair was wild, his beard was like a briar bush, his arms were gnarled as an old apple tree. The servants prodded him forward uncertainly.

"This," announced Hohlmund, "or what remains of it, is, or once was, Veit of Furstenberg, the last of our neighbors. He used to be known as the best archer in the country, but he refused to join us. We met on the field. We fought. He lay at my feet."

Without turning his head or lifting his head, Veit spoke. "We met—by accident. We fought—I had no weapons while you were fully armed. I lay at your feet asking no mercy—welcoming the thrust of your spear."

"But it never came," said Hohlmund. "I preferred to add you to the other beasts in my menagerie. They tell me you were the keenest bowman in the world before you were captured." He turned to the men and women. "At least that was his reputation before his eyes were more or less painlessly removed."

A shudder went through the hall. Veit said, "I can still see some things without my eyes."

"So I have heard," said Hohlmund. "The keepers call you the bat. They tell me that you can locate things by the sound. We shall see if that it true. Remove his chains," he said to the servants.

Hohlmund went to the table. "I have here a silver goblet," he said to the blinded man. "It is being carried to one side of the room— I won't say which side. Someone will strike the goblet twice. If you hit it I will let you go free. If you miss it—" He left the sentence ominously incomplete.

Someone handed Veit a bow and a quiver of arrows. The sightless man ran his hand over the length of the wood and fitted an arrow to the string. A bell-like sound rang through the room. Before it stopped ringing, Veit faced about, let the arrow fly, and the silver goblet clattered to the ground.

"Well done, old bat," said Hohlmund. "Now let the blind bat—"

He got no further. He never spoke again. The sightless bowman sent a second dart toward the sound of the voice. Hohlmund was pinned to the wall. The arrow had gone through his mouth.

THE LORELEY

...*The Siren's Song*

T THE base of a gigantic rock, hundreds of feet below the river Rhine, lies the Rhinegold, the magic hoard which a man might give his soul to possess. And here, at the rock's pinnacle, is the Loreley, the water-witch, who, according to the German poet Heinrich Heine, combs her golden hair and sings a song that lures men fatally to the rock. Seeing her, men forget everything except their dearest dream, the dream of holding in their arms the most beautiful of women. So filmy the watery blue of her robe, so transparent the hue of her skin, she seems nothing more than a condensation of air. Nevertheless, when Loreley opens her arms to lovers, they fall into the Rhine and are never heard of again.

Leonard, the young son of Count Dieterich, had been brought up in his father's castle on the Rhine. He had heard the folktale since his infancy. Nurses had lulled him to sleep with the poem's sliding syllables; harpers had sung ballads about the Loreley and her siren singing. Yet no one had ever seen the face of the Loreley. Leonard resolved not only to look on her face but also to possess her.

On the eve of his twentieth birthday Leonard dressed himself as though for a wedding. He hung a jeweled cross around his neck, left the castle, found a boat, and rowed toward the famous rock. It was a cloudy evening, but gradually the rock defined itself. On the summit, Leonard saw a luminous mist wavering, scarf-like, trailing fold after fold. Then the midst condensed, shaped itself, and took on body —the body of a woman.

Leonard could see everything now: the moon-white skin, the cloud-like arms, the nebulous mouth, the filaments of loosened light

223

that were her hair. He stopped rowing, but the boat did not stop. Waves were impelling it toward the vision. Leonard was unaware of movement, unconscious of everything but the radiance of the Loreley. She began to comb starlight out of her hair and enchantment laid hold on him. She began to sing, and the spell was complete. It was the song he had heard in his heart's heart for years. And now she added a verse.

> The world is full of lovers declaring
>> They'd mount through fire for a single kiss;
> But where is the love that is truly daring,
>> And where is the man who can make me his?

"I am he!" cried Leonard. "I am coming!" And he thrust up a wild arm. Suddenly great waves clutched at the boat, long green hands, pulling it every way at once. Leonard stood up to steady himself, lunged at an oar. But it was too late. The boat, caught in a swirl of rapids, was lifted on the back of a breaker, hung in air for an uncertain moment, and was dashed against the jutting cliff. It split like a nut cracked on a stone. A thin cry went down the wind as the mist cleared and the summit shone with separate stars. All that was ever found to identify Leonard was the jeweled cross, picked up on the bank.

For six weeks Leonard's stricken father spoke to no one. At the end of the seventh week, Dieterich gave orders to his men-at-arms.

"The witch must die," he told them. "Seize her before her magic has power. Do not wait for evening; go early in the day. Mount the cliff before sunset and, when she appears, topple her from the rock. She has haunted the Rhine long enough. Let her be drowned in it."

The afternoon was pleasant, the foothold easy. Ten men climbed to the top. As the sun went down, they formed a close circle about the summit, drew their swords, and rested on their shields. Evening fell and a mist rose. It concentrated upon the peak and disclosed the Loreley in the very center of the armed circle. The men closed in

"What are you here for?" she whispered.

"You!" the leader answered. "You have worked your last enchantment! We are on solid earth and it is not us, but you who will plunge into the Rhine!" And they put their hands upon her.

But fingers caught nothing firmer than space. Wherever they clutched, they missed. She was a dancing light, a will-o'-the-wisp, a moonbeam's ghost, a reflection of an echo. And the phantom sang a new song:

> Father, father, send your waves
> Rough-shod from the deepest caves.
> Strike the waters, make them wild.
> Save your child.

The answering voices were hoarse—voices of winds and waters urging each other on, thunder of waves overtaking the flood, rush of rains meeting them halfway. Floundering upon the height, the warriors saw the river Rhine leave its bed, climb the cliff, and throw itself over the summit. Shields were useless now. Knee-deep in brine they sank in quicksands, grasping at knife-edged rocks, floating weeds, dead twigs. As the Rhine carried them toward the sea, the last man saw the Loreley mount a blue wave that reared like a high-spirited stallion and, tossing its white mane, bear her proudly away.

Since that night, the legend concludes, no one has ever seen the enchantress. But on misty evenings when the moon is full, something of her returns. The Loreley has gone. But her song, repeated by the rock, still calls across the remembering river.

CHANTICLEER

... His Strange Dream

ONG, LONG ago, in a cottage close to a wood, there lived a poor widow. She led a simple life; although she had only a little money she managed to keep herself and her two daughters decently. She had three pigs, three cows, and a sheep she called Nelly. Her kitchen and bedroom were shabby; her food was plain, and she had to work hard for whatever she got. She drank milk with coarse bread, ate a bit of bacon, and sometimes an egg or two.

In her yard, which was enclosed by a fence and a dry ditch, she kept a handsome cock called Chanticleer. When it came to crowing there was no rooster like him. His voice was louder and livelier than the church organ on Sundays, and his crowing was more punctual than any clock. His comb was red as fine coral and notched like a castle wall. His bill was black and shone like jet. His legs and toes were heavenly blue; his nails were lily white; and his feathers were burnished gold. He was the lord of seven hens, but his favorite wife was the winsome Lady Pertelote. She was companionable and courteous, and she was the mistress of Chanticleer's heart. They were always happy together. It was a joy to hear them join in such songs as "My love's far from the land"—for this was in the time when all birds and beasts could speak as well as sing.

One morning, at the break of day, instead of lifting his voice in the usual call, Chanticleer uttered a deep groan. Pertelote, who sat next to him on the perch, was troubled. "What is it, my love?" she asked. "Why do you groan like that? You should be merry and wide awake to herald the new day."

"Don't be angry, my dear," replied Chanticleer. "I have had a strange dream, a dream so terrible that I am still frightened. My heart has not stopped pounding. In this dream I was walking up and down our yard when suddenly I saw a beast inside of it. It was something like a dog, with red and yellow hair, but its ears and tail were tufted with black. Its snout, between two burning eyes, was small and pointed, and it stood there, about to seize and devour me. It was enough to make anyone die of fright."

"Shame!" cried Pertelote. "You talk like a coward, and a coward is someone I cannot love. No matter what she may say, every woman wants her husband to be sturdy, brave, and free of fear. How can you tell me that there is anything on earth to make you tremble! Haven't you a man's heart to match your manly beard! As for your dream—all dreams are nonsense. They mean nothing but that you've eaten too much. Take something for your stomach; a good laxative will do you a world of good. I will make a dose for you from herbs in our own barnyard—hellebore root, creeping ivy, thornberries, laurel—mixed with a few worms. Swallow it right down, and I promise you'll never again be afraid to dream any kind of dream!"

"Thank you," said Chanticleer. "I'm sure it will make me feel better. Just the same, there are lots of people—famous writers, too— who have believed in dreams. They claimed that dreams foretell all sorts of things good and bad. The Bible is full of dreamers. Remember Joseph who rose to glory after he interpreted the dreams of Pharaoh, king of Egypt. And don't forget the legend of Croesus, king of Lydia, who dreamed that he was perched high in a tree— and it was on a tree that he was hanged. Then there was the wife of Hector, the Trojan warrior. She dreamed that if Hector went into battle he would be killed, and, as you know, he refused to listen to her and was slain by Achilles. I could go on and on. Just let me say that the dream I had gives me reason to fear some ill fortune."

Pertelote looked unhappy and Chanticleer hastened to change the subject. "Don't worry about me. I have much to be thankful for," he said. "When I look at you and see how lovely you are, all my fears vanish. It is then I know the truth of the proverb: 'Woman is man's delight and all his bliss.' When you are at my side I am so full of joy I can laugh at everything, even the worst dream."

With these words Chanticleer flew down from his perch and, with a loud cluck, summoned his flock. He showed his hens the corn he had found, lovingly guided Pertelote, and, lordly as a lion, strutted up and down. He was so proud that his toes scarcely touched the ground. Every time he spied another kernel he clucked happily, and all his wives came running.

Thirty-two days after the end of March, Chanticleer, attended by his seven wives, looked up at the brilliant sun and crowed triumphantly. "See!" he cried. "Behold how the sun has climbed the heaven. Listen, my Pertelote, hear how joyfully the birds salute the day, and see how cheerfully the flowers spring up! My heart has never been so full of gayety!"

At that very moment something terrible happened. A black fox, the slyest of his kind, had been prowling about the woods. Breaking through the hedge, he had squeezed through the fence that enclosed the yard in which Chanticleer and his hens were housed. There he lay in a stony bed, hidden by the herbs, waiting for the moment when he could pounce. The hens were basking in the sun; Pertelote was enjoying a dust-bath; and Chanticleer was singing like a mermaid in the sea.

Suddenly his eye saw something among the herbs that almost stopped his heart. He saw the fox crouching low and, although he had no desire to crow, he warned the hens and, when they scurried away, Chanticleer turned to flee. But the fox stood up and, barring his way, addressed him. He was very courteous.

"Why in such a hurry?" asked the fox suavely. "I am your friend —surely you can't be afraid of me! I did not come here to spy on you or disturb your privacy in any way; I came here only in the hope of hearing you sing. It is known that you have a voice as sweet as any of the angels who sing in the choirs of heaven. I never heard such a singer as your father. He sang from the heart; every note he struck was full and clear. He would stand on his tiptoes, close his eyes, stretch his neck, and let the music pour out. You are his son, and it would delight me to hear what they say, that you sound exactly like him. Won't you give me the pleasure?"

Chanticleer could not resist this shameless flattery. He raised his head, clapped his wings, stretched his neck, shut his eyes, and crowed at the top of his voice. The fox did not lose a second. He sprang at Chanticleer, caught him by the throat, slung him across his back, and ran off. For the moment there was no pursuit.

An instant later there was a great outburst. The hens cried as wildly as did the wives of the warriors at the fall of Troy. Loudly they wailed, Pertelote most of all. Their shrieks were like the frightful sounds heard when Nero set fire to Rome and the women wept and screamed helplessly while their husbands perished in the flames.

Hearing the frantic noise, the widow and her two daughters rushed out of doors. Catching sight of Chanticleer being carried off, they shouted, "Help! Help!" Others came running. Sticks and stones began to fly. Dogs and cats ran into the road; calves and hogs squealed and bellowed. Ducks flew out of the water quacking; geese honked over the trees. The crowd became a yelling mob as bees left their hives and buzzed angrily about people's heads. Trumpets were blown, horns blared, brasses were banged. There were prolonged howls, roars, hoots, brays, blasts, squeals, squawks, screeches, yells, whoops, and continual caterwauling until it seemed that the heavens were crashing to earth.

Suddenly fortune, which had favored the fox, turned against him. In spite of his danger, the cock managed to find a voice. "Sir," he quacked, "if I were you, I would face that crowd. A brave creature like you should shout defiantly: 'Turn back! Now that I have reached the woods, shout your loudest, do your worst! The cock is mine—I'll eat him soon enough!'"

"You're right," replied the fox. "That's exactly what I'll do!"

Opening his mouth to speak, he let go of Chanticleer's throat, and the cock flew into a tall tree. "Alas, my Chanticleer," said the fox smoothly, "I seem to have done wrong. I'm afraid I may have frightened you when I rushed you from the yard and held you too tight. But, really, I meant no harm. Come down here. Let me explain."

"No, thank you," said the cock. "Never again will I let flattery make me open my mouth and close my eyes. Anyone who blinks his eyes when he should keep them wide open and his mouth shut deserves whatever he gets."

WAT TYLER

...The Peasants' Revolt

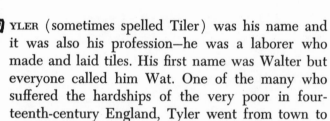 TYLER (sometimes spelled Tiler) was his name and it was also his profession—he was a laborer who made and laid tiles. His first name was Walter but everyone called him Wat. One of the many who suffered the hardships of the very poor in fourteenth-century England, Tyler went from town to town looking for work. In the county of Kent he heard a priest, John Ball, preaching in the marketplace. The archbishop had forbidden anyone to preach outside of the church, but Ball ignored the order.

"You are bondsmen, which means you are slaves, for you are bound to do what you are told to do and never complain," Ball told his listeners. "You must plow the fields for others, you must harvest the grain for others, carry it to the barns, thrash and winnow it, and do all things for others without payment. You are not merely peasants but slaves of the lords who own the land. When the world began there were no slaves, but that is what you have become. All men are descended from the same parents, Adam and Eve, and all are born equal. Yet today the country is run by masters who treat you like beasts. When you do not perform the services they require, you are beaten or thrown into prison. You are many; they are few. Shame upon you that you do not resist. Are you too timid to do something?"

Wat Tyler spoke up. "What *can* we do?" he asked.

"You can gather in numbers," replied Ball. "You can show strength. You can go to the king and demand your rights. You can demand freedom."

Wat went along with Ball. Crowds collected wherever Ball spoke. They knew he spoke the truth. Their numbers increased by the hundreds. Soon there were a thousand, then ten thousand, then twenty thousand. They became an army, a very ragged army, but, nevertheless, a threatening force. Ball was arrested. The archbishop would have put him to death for defying him, but he feared the anger of the people. After several months Ball was released. He continued preaching.

"Not content to work you until you drop," he said, "the lords of the land are taxing you to death. You are taxed for the food you eat, for the clothes you wear, for the few feet of ground on which you sleep and in which you'll be buried. Now there is an added tax, a new tax to pay the cost of a war with France—a tax so that you can go abroad and be killed. We must stop all this. We must march on London and talk to the king."

The march began. Wat Tyler was chosen as leader. Wherever they went their numbers grew. Every county hailed Ball and Tyler as heralds of a new freedom. The mutterings of discontent became a peasants' revolt. By the time the marchers reached London, it was an organized rebellion of sixty thousand men and women.

The king, Richard the Second, a boy of fourteen, and his advisors agreed to a parley with the peasants. But when the king and his court saw how many there were and how fierce they looked, a meeting was refused. The marchers were angered. They shouted, threw stones, broke windows, and lost all control of themselves. They turned into mobs bent on damage. They set fire to houses, looted shops, demolished prisons and set the prisoners free. People were struck down; killings were common. The revolt was country-wide. They sacked Canterbury and murdered the archbishop. A kind of madness swept over everyone; the rebellion became a riot.

Finally the king and his advisors consented to meet the leaders of the uprising. They chose a place outside of London called Mile End. The young king spoke.

"What is it you want?" he asked.

"We want one thing more than anything," replied Wat. "We want our freedom."

"I grant your wish," said the king. "Return to your homes, and I shall have papers drawn up that will satisfy you all."

Many of the peasants were appeased and thousands of them left the scene. But half their number—more than thirty thousand—were distrustful. Wat addressed those who remained.

"Words do not move me," he said. "A promise is not enough. I will not be convinced until the promise is performed. Let us wait."

They waited, but nothing happened to assure them that reforms would be carried out. The people were still forced to work for their masters without recompense. When conditions did not change and grew, if anything, worse, Wat called his followers together again. Thousands of them intercepted the king in front of the abbey of St. Bartholomew in Smithfield. Young Richard was attended by a troop of horsemen together with the Lord Mayor of London and his staff, all seemingly unarmed but with weapons concealed under their robes.

"What is the meaning of this?" said the king. "Did I not grant your request? Did I not give you my word?"

"You gave us your word," replied Wat. "But that is all you gave us. Words will not free us. There must be deeds. Not later, but now. If no one acts for us, we will act for ourselves."

"Insolence!" said the Lord Mayor. "You speak like a traitor!"

"I speak for the people," said Wat, raising his hand in protest.

No one knew whether the gesture was a demand for attention or a signal. It was a tense moment.

"The traitor has condemned himself!" cried the Lord Mayor. "He has dared to raise his hand against his majesty. Seize him!"

Before he could defend himself, Wat was thrown to the ground. Drawing a sword from his robe, the Lord Mayor struck at Tyler. The attendants flashed their weapons and stabbed Wat to death.

Bewildered at what they saw, the peasants broke ranks, scattered, and fled. The king's soldiers pursued them and those that did not surrender were slaughtered. Ball was captured and killed. His head and Tyler's were stuck on poles and displayed on London Bridge. What had begun as a vision of freedom ended in a nightmare of violence.

Historians have not agreed about Wat Tyler. To some he seems a miscreant, to others a martyr. "O liberty," cried Madame Roland, who was executed during the French revolution, "O liberty, what crimes are committed in thy name!"

GUY FAWKES

...*The Gunpowder Plot*

UY FAWKES was an English Catholic who, with many others of his faith, felt that his Catholic countrymen were cruelly oppressed. The cry of "No Popery! No Popery!" rang through the early years of the seventeenth century in England, and Catholics were victimized. Guy Fawkes had been a soldier honored for bravery and he considered himself a coward for doing nothing when so many of his fellow-religionists were wronged.

When the House of Lords passed severe laws against what was called "the evil bondage of Roman superstition," Guy Fawkes met with a group of Catholic laymen.

"We are being treated as though we were dogs—verminous dogs," he said angrily. "We are accused of treason if we try to persuade anyone that ours is holy faith. We are never received at court. We are not even allowed within ten miles of London unless we happen to be tradesmen. We are not permitted to become lawyers or doctors or hold any office in the government. It is time for us to show that we are citizens with the same rights as other Englishmen. We must do something, something drastic."

"What would you suggest?" asked one of the group.

"Let us strike at the source where they make the laws," said Guy Fawkes. "Let us destroy the House of Lords."

"But how can it be done?" they asked. "The place is heavily guarded."

"We would not try to attack the parliament from the outside. We would work from the inside. We would hire the house next door. Then we would dig a tunnel between the cellar and the cellar of the

House of Lords. While others work, making the mine and bringing in barrels of gunpowder, I would act as sentinel. It should not take too long."

All agreed, and all were sworn to secrecy. The house next to the House of Lords was hired, the tunnel was dug, and thirty-six barrels of gunpowder weighing over a ton were placed in the cellar directly beneath the House of Lords. The barrels were covered with coal and iron bars in order to conceal them and also to give more force to the explosion. A slow fuse was attached so that, after it was lit, Guy Fawkes would have time to escape before the place blew up.

Everything was in readiness for the blow. It was scheduled for November 6, 1604. However, the day before it was to occur one of the conspirators "leaked" the information. The plot was discovered; the suspects were seized and held for questioning. Guy Fawkes refused to give the names of his accomplices or, when they were brought to trial, to testify against them. He was tortured, condemned,

and executed. Someone wrote a rude rhyme and stuck it on his grave.

> Lie there, lie there, till you're rotten.
> Soon, Guy Fawkes, you'll be forgotten.

The rhyme was wrong. Guy Fawkes was not forgotten. On the contrary, he was celebrated through the centuries, although not in the way he might have wished. November 5th, the day of the discovery of the Gunpowder Plot, is a time for merrymaking in England. Boys and girls dress up in outlandish costumes supposed to suggest Guy Fawkes—this is how the word "guy" came into being—and the night is gay with fireworks. The climax of the celebration is the parading of a stuffed figure representing Guy Fawkes, after which the dummy is burned.

But what Guy Fawkes did, or failed to do, is immortalized in—of all places—Mother Goose. There it stands, a jingle that echoes in the mind.

> Please to remember
> The fifth of November,
>   Gunpowder treason and plot.
> I see no reason
> Why gunpowder treason
>   Should ever be forgot.

MIGHTY MICHAEL

...*Who Could Do Anything*

VERY country has its folklore about gigantic heroes, oversize men who perform fabulous feats. Greece had the invincible Herakles, America has Paul Bunyan, the demi-god of the lumber camps, and Europe has his counterpart in the legendary Mighty Michael.

Doing the impossible was child's play for Mighty Michael. He had been doing it since he was a child. When he was five years old he heard his father, a hard-working farmer, complaining to his mother.

"Three times a week I have to bring our market stuff to town. The road is so curved and crooked that it takes me twice as long to get there as it should. Also it's so hilly, so fully of holes and bumps, that every time I leave home I wear out the horse as well as myself."

"Too bad," said his wife. "But you can't expect a road to straighten itself. And no one could do it for you."

Little Michael—he wasn't called Mighty then—spoke up, "I can do it," he said.

His mother and father laughed. "He likes to make little jokes," said his father. Michael smiled and said nothing more. But that evening after supper he went out, took hold of one end of the road, and pulled. For a minute or two nothing happened. He pulled harder and harder. Suddenly there was a creaking sound, the sound of something ripping itself loose, and the road tore free from the earth.

"There," he said to his father the next morning. "There's your road. I had to pull it over to one side, and I had to flatten it a little. But it's straight now.

Michael grew up fast, and he grew up big, bigger than any man in Europe. He was fifteen when he earned the name of Mighty. The village needed a new church, but the men were too busy to build one. Besides, there was no lumber-yard to supply the material.

"Let me do it for you," said Michael. "It won't take long."

This time his father did not laugh and Michael walked down the road he had straightened. Near the end of the road, on the outskirts of the town, was a forest. Michael went in, seized two of the tallest trees, and tore them up by the roots. Then he tore up two more, and more, and more, until he had a whole lumberyard of timber. Putting them on his back, he brought the lot to the village, shredded the trees, and broke them across his knee as if they were twigs. Next he fitted them together as if he were building a toy house, drove in nails, made doors and windows, and added the tallest steeple the villagers had ever seen.

"You will have to make your own pews," he told them. "I can't handle small things."

Then a time came when the able-bodied men had to serve as soldiers and were called away to war. Worst of all, it happened at harvest time. What would be done with the fields of wheat and oats and corn and barley which were ripe and needing to be gathered? The women looked anxiously at Mighty Michael.

"Don't worry," he said. "Get me the longest sword you can find and get ready to do the gleaning."

When he got the sword, he brought down a towering pine. Setting the sword-blade at an angle to the wooden shaft of the tree he made an enormous scythe. With this he reaped all the fields—there were a hundred acres of them—in a single day.

By the time the men returned from war, Mighty Michael had become the idol of the village. The women's admiration was so great it was bound to cause jealousy. A few of the men met secretly.

"He is winning our women away from us," they said. "If we don't do something he will rule us all. He must be stopped—now!"

They came to Mighty Michael asking his help.

"The spring rains have caused a lot of flooding and the river is so swollen that the town is in danger," they said. "You are the only one who can save us."

"But how?" asked Michael.

"By removing the stuff—limbs of trees, broken parts of barns, roots, and rocks—that the river has washed down. You are the one who can do it. They don't call you Mighty Michael for nothing."

"Right gladly," said Michael. "I'll do it right away."

The men hid in the woods, and when Michael waded into the stream, they threw huge stones at him. A few hit him, but he only grinned.

"It's a fine day," he said, "yet pieces of hail seem to be falling from a clear sky."

Desperately the men aimed a heavy millstone at his head. Michael caught it in midair, stuck his head through the hole, and put it around his neck.

"Not only hail but fine presents seem to be dropping down. Thanks," he said, raising his head to the heavens. "People will envy my handsome collar."

This, however, was not the end of Michael's troubles. The men continued to plot against him. They persuaded more and more men of the village to join them; they made a plan to get rid of him. One of the women came to him secretly.

"You have been good to us," she said, "but the men will not let you live to be called Mighty Michael. A hundred of them have surrounded the town and have sworn to kill you if you try to escape. I do not know what you can do. They swear they will seize you no matter how fast you walk, run, or leap."

"Thank you," said Mighty Michael, "and don't worry. I will think of a way. I won't have to walk or run or leap, but I *will* get out and no one will stop me."

Next morning he tied a rabbit to a stake. Soon an eagle spied the rabbit and swooped to snatched his prey. Mighty Michael was the one who did the snatching, for he caught and killed the eagle. Then he fastened the eagle's wings to his strongest horse, sprang on the horse's back, and flew over the heads of the men who were lying in wait for him.

"Keep on waiting till you catch something," he shouted to them. "You'll never catch Mighty Michael."

He never was seen again. At least he was never seen again on earth. However, on certain hot summer evenings when clouds gather and the air presses close and low thunder is heard, flashes of light open and shut in the sky. Some people call it heat lightning. But others say it is Mighty Michael flying, flying to his heavenly home.

BEATRICE

... And the Statue

IT WAS A modest cloister that nestled in the woods, and the nuns that lived there matched their unpretentious surroundings. The quietest and the humblest was Sister Beatrice. She was the cloister's caretaker, as retiring as she was hard working. She tended the choir, polished the brass rail of the altar, waxed the woodwork, kept the statue of the Virgin spotless, and arose every morning before the sun was up to ring the bell that called the nuns to prayer.

There were a few moments in the day when she had nothing to do and no prayers to say. At such times she would lean over the convent walls and gaze at the colored fields below. She saw, far off and tiny as in a doll's dream, another sort of life pass on the little, twisting roads. She watched great princes ride with their gaily-colored court and saw the gypsies rambling along in the early dusk. She caught glimpses of laughing adventurers, shields flashing and swords sparkling in the sunlight. She heard the neighing of young horses, the horn of the hunter in the woods, and the answering shout of men. And her heart filled with longing for the world. In these moments she felt shut in—the convent seemed a prison—and she would have given everything to be on that bright and lively road. Then, rousing herself, she would go back to her tasks and work harder than ever, especially when she tended the beloved statue of the Virgin.

But one day in early summer the world was so full of beauty that Sister Beatrice could not take her eyes or her thoughts away from it. That night she could not sleep. After tossing about until it was almost morning, she arose and, by the blue light of a July moon, put on her clothes and her strongest pair of shoes. As she passed through the chapel, she stopped before the altar and, kneeling in front of the statue of the Virgin, she said, "I have served you faithfully for many years, have loved you deeply, but I can serve you no longer. My life lies elsewhere. Take the keys from me, for I am no longer worthy to carry them." And, with a prayer, she laid her keys in the hand of the statue and went out into the summer night.

The stars were still in the sky as Sister Beatrice went down the mountain and found the high road. No one was there except a frightened rabbit or a fox running across the path. She walked until she was weary and then, as she came to a crossroad in the woods, sat down to rest beside a stone trough in which a mountain spring was bubbling. There she stayed until the sun arose and the dew glistened on her hair like diamonds scattered over silk.

As the first rays of the sun shot through the trees, they fell on a knight in full armor riding alone. The nun, who, since childhood, had never seen a man so close, stared at him with wide-open eyes. As she never moved a muscle, the knight took her for a statue and would have ridden past her if his ear had not caught the sound of falling water. The tinkle of the spring made him turn his horse around and allow him to drink. It was then that the knight realized the figure was a living woman. Hastily dismounting, he bowed to the lovely nun and asked if he could be of any service to her. He was a crusader, he told her, and, having lost all his people after a long absence in the Holy Land, he was returning home.

While he talked, he looked straight into Beatrice's eyes, and she returned his gaze as though she had never seen anything so wonderful. At last he inquired which way she was going and offered his services again.

Then Beatrice told him everything. She told him how she had longed for other things and had run away from the convent to see the world. "But now," she ended, "I am frightened and do not know what to do."

"If you will go with me," he answered, without taking his eyes from her lovely face, "I will be your guide wherever you wish to go and will be your true knight always. My castle is only one day's journey from here. There you can be at home and afterward, if you still wish to see more of the world, I will provide you with horse and help and all you may need."

This gallant speech so pleased her that she lost all fear. Without saying yes or no, she allowed him to lift her on his horse. He swung himself on the saddle behind her, and off they rode through forest and field.

It was not long before these two, who had fallen in love with each other at first sight, ceased to watch the changing landscape and spoke of nothing but their happiness. They had not ridden three hours before he had asked her to marry him and she, with a kiss, had promised to be his bride. Her hands were clasped in his; her head was on his shoulder; she looked at nothing else but him. And so she, who had longed to see the wide world, cared for no greater part of it than what this horse was carrying.

Gayheart, the knight, also thought of nothing else until he saw the towers of his father's castle shining in the setting sun. It was late evening before they reached the gates, and the moon coming from behind the high walls gave the only light there was. The castle was dark outside, darker still within the courtyard. Gayheart's father and mother had died and all the servants had gone except one old steward, who finally came to the door. Scarcely able to speak with joy at seeing his young master again, he ushered them in, bowing and falling over himself in his excitement. In spite of his age the old steward had kept everything in good condition. The rooms were always ready for the master's return, the woodwork shone, the tapestries were like new. Soon an inviting supper stood upon the table and Gayheart and Beatrice sat down to their first meal together.

The marriage was to take place in a few weeks. The steward found some young country-people to take the place of the former servants and great preparations were made. Gayheart opened his mother's large chest and took out silks and laces and jewels and gorgeous costumes by the dozen. Beatrice tried them all, and each one looked lovelier on her than the other.

One day, about a week before the wedding, a foreign baron came to the castle with his followers. He had met Gayheart during the crusades and a feast was arranged in honor of the visitor. After the dinner there were songs and stories and games of all sorts. Finally, just before the end, they started to throw dice and gamble for money, horses, and other valuables. Gayheart was lucky; he won almost every turn. But the baron was not to be discouraged. "Come," he said, "though luck is on your side, let us try one more throw. And, as this is the last one, let us gamble for something worth while. What is the most valuable thing you have?"

Gayheart thought a moment. Then he said, smiling, "My beautiful Beatrice."

"Good," said the baron. "Against her I will set my entire castle with all it contains, as well as the farms and hunting-park surrounding it. What do you say?"

For a moment Gayheart hesitated. First he thought it was only a jest. Then, when he saw the baron was in earnest, he thought how good fortune had favored him in everything. Besides (he said to himself) it would be a pleasant surprise to give the baron's huge estate to Beatrice for a wedding present. Therefore, with a confident laugh, he cried, "So be it!" took up the dice, threw them on the board —and lost.

With that the baron stood up, seized Beatrice by the hand, and called his men to ride forth at once. Gayheart, who had collapsed into his chair, sat as if stunned, while the baron gave hurried orders for departure. It had all happened so quickly that Beatrice—who had been out of the room when the wager was made and who came too late to prevent it—had barely time to kiss Gayheart and, weeping bitterly, hide the unlucky dice in the bosom of her dress.

The baron and his company had not ridden more than an hour when they came to a little cluster of white birches with a brook rippling besides them. Overhead the branches, meeting each other, made a green tent, while the slender tree-trunks seemed silver poles that held it high. Here the baron chose to rest, and it was here that Beatrice first spoke to him.

"And now that you have me, what do you intend to do, my lord?" she asked.

"I shall take you to my castle and marry you as soon as we enter its doors," replied the baron. "I won you in fair play and you are mine."

"You won my body," replied Beatrice. "You did not win my heart. Rather than be married against my will, I would kill myself here!"

"You would not do such a terrible thing," cried the baron. "It is a sin to take one's own life!"

"It is also a sin to compel me, by force, to marry you," responded Beatrice. "But," she continued in a quieter voice, "I will make a bargain with you. If you really want me, you must play with higher stakes than your castle. Will you risk your life against my love?"

As she said this, her color rose, while the baron noticed only how proud and beautiful she was. Scarcely understanding her words, he nodded his head. "Then," continued Beatrice, "let us gamble once more. If I win, I am to be free and you must surrender your life to me. If you win, I promise to do as you wish and obey you in all things. Give me your sword, and here"—taking the dice from her bosom—"let the dice decide."

Still half bewitched by her beauty, the baron handed over his sword, grasped the dice and, rattling them fiercely together, threw the next to the highest number in one throw. "Eleven!" he shouted, and smiled at Beatrice in triumph. Beatrice, taking the dice in her hand and breathing a hurried prayer, rolled them gently on the ground. "Twelve!" gasped the baron, staring first at the dice and then at her as though she were an enchantress.

"You may keep your life. I do not want it," said Beatrice, and, curtsying to him, stuck his sword under her arm and ran off in the direction they had come. As the dumbfounded baron kept staring after her, she turned a curve in the road less than fifty feet from where he was standing but, instead of keeping on, Beatrice did a crafty thing. She left the path and hid herself behind a clump of bushes and small trees that grew so thick that, even from the road, it was impossible to see her. She stood still as a stone deer; a sparkling sunbeam falling on one of the jewels in her necklace was the only thing about her that moved. The baron saw this shining but, still in a daze, thought it was nothing more than the glistening of a drop of dew and paid no attention to it.

Finally he roused himself and blew furiously on his hunting-horn. As his men came running up, he threw himself on his horse and, calling on them to follow, flew in pursuit of his escaped prize. "Bring her back!" he shouted. "She cannot have got far by this time. Bring her back!"

About an hour later they came back, slowly and sullenly, scarcely holding themselves straight as they rode through the silver birches while the magpies chattered mockingly in the branches. As soon as they had passed, Beatrice came out of her hiding-place and hurried home, making no attempt to spare her fine clothes and delicate shoes as she ran over the rough road across stony fields.

Meanwhile Gayheart had been spending many unhappy hours. Torn by anger and regret, he reproached himself for his stupid folly. "What a fool I was!" he groaned. "What have I done! I have lost her—the one thing I love most in the world—and now I know that I cannot live without her. What have I done?" he cried again, burying his face in his hands. All of a sudden he had the feeling that someone else was in the room and, looking up, he saw, to his amazed surprise, it was she. Tears and laughter mingled as he took her in his arms and she told how she had escaped from the baron.

To guard against other accidents, they were married at once. Beatrice became the most beloved lady for miles around. She was always visiting the workers on her husband's estate, helping the mothers, making presents to the children. In the neighboring castles no feast or hunt was complete without her. She was adored by the rich and worshiped by the poor.

The years came and went with changing fortunes and, after many harvests had been gathered, Beatrice was the mother of eight handsome sons, who grew up like young deer.

The oldest boy had just turned eighteen when a strange thing happened. Beatrice awoke one autumn night with the new moon shining in her eyes. It was as if a voice had called her, calling from a great distance. For awhile she lay there without moving, but with her eyes wide open, as though her whole body were listening. Then she arose, carefully put away all her jewels and fine clothes, locked the great chest which contained them and placed the key in the hands of the sleeping Gayheart. With naked feet she went to where her sons were sleeping, said a prayer for each and kissed them softly, one after another. At last she came back to her husband's bed, laid a long kiss on his forehead, put on a coarse gown which she wore when she had deserted the convent, and, silently, as a ghost, left the castle. A cold wind was howling and the falling leaves pelted her as she plodded on toward the convent she had left years ago.

She walked without stopping to rest until she came to the convent gate and there, with a faint heart, she knocked for admittance. In a few moments the old door-keeper let her in and greeted her by name as casually as though she had been away on some little errand. Unable to understand this, Beatrice, whose heart was still beating loudly, went into the chapel and threw herself at the altar before the statue of the Virgin. Suddenly circles of light appeared about the Holy Mother and her infant. Then the statue spoke.

"You have been away a rather long time, my daughter," said the statue. "But I know your heart. I know you have never forgotten me. I did not forget you. I have taken your place as care-taker all this time and have performed your daily tasks these twenty years. But I am glad you have returned, and now you can have your keys again."

The statue bent down and gave Beatrice the keys, while the nun was filled with frightened wonder at this miracle. Breathing a swift prayer, Beatrice went about her tasks at once, did this and that and the other thing, and when the bell rang for lunch, she went in to table. Many of the nuns had grown old, others had died, younger ones had come, and a new abbess sat at the head of the table. Beatrice sat in her usual place, just as if she had never set foot outside of the convent walls. No one noticed anything strange about her being there—nobody even knew she had been away—for, when the Virgin took her place, she also took on the appearance of the absent nun.

Some years later the nuns celebrated a great holiday at the convent. It was a most important occasion and it had been decided that each of the nuns was to give the Virgin as beautiful a present as she could make. One of them had woven an exquisite cloth to lay upon the altar; another had embroidered a gorgeous banner; the third one had made a long robe of gold brocade. One composed a Latin hymn; another set it to music; a third wrote out and decorated a book of prayers. Everybody made something: a painting or a poem or a piece of lace. Those who could do nothing else sewed a new shirt for the Christ-child and the sister-cook baked him a plate of cookies. Beatrice was the only one who had nothing ready. Possibly because she was too tired, possibly because her thoughts were more in the past than in the present—whatever the reason may have been, Beatrice could think of nothing to give the Virgin.

It was the morning of the great celebration. The chapel, smelling of incense and fresh flowers, sparkled with hundreds of candles as the nuns walked past and laid their offerings on the altar or at the feet of the statue. Only Beatrice hung back, having nothing to offer. She stood timidly to one side while the bells pealed and the incense-smoke curled toward Heaven.

As her turn came, the door sprang open and a company of mounted knights was seen, their shields blazing in the sunlight. They stood there, a small army on their proud horses, until their leader, a gray old crusader, commanded them to dismount. He had come, he explained, with his eight sons on the way to the Holy Land and had stopped here to pray to the Virgin for good fortune. The entire company entered—the father, the eight sons, and their pages—and the nuns marveled at the beautiful picture as the noble-looking graybeard kneeled with his eight young heroes looking like so many young gods in full armor. As they removed their helmets, Beatrice recognized Gayheart and her children and cried out to them. Gathering each one in turn to her breast, she told her secret and related what had been performed for her sake by the Virgin. "And now,"

she said, "I do not have to come before my Helper with empty hands, for I have eight great gifts to offer. Accept, most holy Lady, my eight sons, whose lives will glorify thee."

Everyone could see that this, the richest of the presents, was accepted. For, suddenly, the chapel was full of the sound of great wings. An angel stood in air above each of the sons, while eight wreaths appeared on the heads of the young men, eight crowns of green oak-leaves with acorns of pure gold. "A miracle!" cried the astonished nuns. "A miracle!"

Beatrice, in the midst of her boys, and the statue of the Virgin, holding her babe, smiled at each other.

THE ESKIMO WIDOW

...And Her Strange Son

I N THE coldest part of the Arctic zone, the Eskimos have a legend they tell when the long winter nights are at their worst. It is about a little old woman who lived in the northernmost part of Alaska and who lived alone. Her husband had died years ago, and her only son had never returned from a long bear hunt. Unable to do her own hunting or fishing, she lived on what her neighbors gave her. It was a poor village; the neighbors had little to spare; and most of the time she was as hungry as she was lonely.

One morning she heard a queer noise that sounded like a child crying. When she could no longer ignore it, she went outside and found a huddle of matted fur on the ice. It was a baby polar bear whose mother had been caught and who had managed to crawl away before the hunters could kill it. Its helplessness moved her lonely heart. Without thinking how she might provide for him, she carried him in and gave him some scraps she had been saving for her next meal. He licked them up eagerly, yawned, and fell asleep.

Now she was no longer alone. Remembering her lost son, she cared for the cub as though he were her child. She gave him half of what little food she got, and, as a result, she was hungrier than ever. But she was happy. Once in a while, when the Eskimos made a great catch, everyone in the village was given part of it, and the old woman and her cub would feast for a few days. Most of the time, however, everyone went hungry.

Somehow the old woman survived and, somehow, the cub got chubby. Then he grew lean and tall. One day, after he had become the most important thing in her life, he disappeared. That night the old woman could not sleep. "My son! My son!" she moaned. Next morning she cried again, but this time it was a cry of joy. Her cub had returned with a fine catch of salmon. He had taught himself how to fish.

As he grew up, he became a clever hunter. No longer a cub, the young bear caught not only fish but, once in a while, a small seal. There was plenty now for both of them. Soon there was enough to share with the neighbors. Everyone remarked what a smart bear he was. "My son," she repeated proudly.

But the good days did not last long. Suddenly the weather changed. For weeks blinding snow-storms swept over the village. Not a fish could be caught; the seals seemed to have swum away.

It was then that one of the men had a plan. "Why should we starve," he said, "when we have food right here? The old woman's bear has plenty of flesh beneath that fur. It should make good eating."

The others said nothing, but they plowed grimly through shoulder-high snowdrifts to the old woman's house. There they found the widow weeping. The bear had disappeared again.

The men slunk to their homes. There was nothing to say, nothing to do. The storms grew worse; there seemed no hope for the starving village.

Then one day the wind shifted and the bear came back. Every-one stared at him. No one spoke. The widow, a little bundle of bones, was too weak to call out, but she managed a cracked smile. The bear did not stir from where he stood, but he lifted his head again and again.

"He's trying to tell us something," said one of the men.

"I think he wants us to go with him," said one of the others. "He seems to be pointing."

The bear shuffled off; the men followed. He led them over hum-mocks, skirting wide cracks and deep crevices. Finally he stopped. A hundred yards in front of him, there was a dark mass barely moving on an ice floe. As they came closer the men saw it was a wounded but still ferocious animal, a huge bull seal, larger than anyone had ever caught. Here was food to last a long, long time— plenty of meat and an endless supply of blubber, the precious fat that would put new life into the entire village. They went to work. It was a small but triumphant procession that brought back the food and the bear. Both were welcomed, especially the bear.

"He knew what we needed," the people told each other, "and he found it for us."

"He didn't just find it," said one of the men, "he fought it for us. We owe everything to him."

"We owe everything to him," the people repeated. "And we owe him to one we will never forget."

The widow waited until the bear walked over and put his muzzle in her hand. Then she patted the shaggy head. "My son," she said softly.